Death

of a

Spaceman

by Sonny Wareham

ISBN: 978-0-692-20754-3

Dedication

For Meg, the greatest gal in the galaxy...

Chapter One

ZZKKTTT-WWHRRR!!!

A din filled the cavern behind my artificial eyes. The quacks said that it was impossible, there could be no sound, but that is what I heard. And I knew I could trust my hearing.

Zzkktt-whhrrr!

I saw spots, although I hadn't yet opened my eyelids. One by one, a million sensory pinpoints bloomed. Through the full spectrum of colors, the pixels phased from infrared through ultraviolet and beyond. I saw each one as they burst like an old stop-action vid of a flower blossoming to life, accompanied by a tiny poof and the acrid smell of burning sulfur. The White Coats said that this was impossible, too, and it was only my imagination filling in sensory information. They were probably right about that.

Zzzkkkkttt -

My sight awakened, but I kept my eyes closed. My proximity sensors and auditory reactors already gave me the details of the building. I knew that it was three stories tall with a cavernous basement below the inadequately supported floor. The room was roughly seventy-two cubic meters and was occupied by eighty-six people – not "people", but "Shoorulians", however since they were roughly humanoid, I gave 'em the benefit of the doubt – twenty-seven were in this barroom; three were in a backroom preparing a greasy fare of gruel which was probably the source of the seaweed stench that we smelled a couple of blocks away; ten were on the second floor, mostly prone and inactive; two were doing something mysterious in a cramped attic space above; and one was in one of the small adjoining rooms being violently ill – which also might be the source of the seaweed stench; and then there were two humans: Stosh and Me.

Yes, and I didn't wait to open my eyes to savor the grog they served here which was a thick, hickory-flavored ale, probably the reason the inn is so well-populated. You can travel the galaxy and delight in the variety of delicacies that innumerable species on planets far and wide have to offer, but damned few beings brew a really good beer. Or so The Old Man said.

Stosh and I had worked together for about five standard years. He was an observant human himself but couldn't match my talents. My erstwhile "seeing-eye dog", I already knew more about the room than Stosh did – the mass of the building materials, the critical architectural stress points and even the chemical composition of the tasty beer they served. All that before I opened my eyes.

A slight nudge from Stosh indicated that it was safe to scan the room. Still, I kept my eyes closed. Parabolic sensors scanned numerous conversations, picked out individual whistles from the buzz of the room. The Shoorulian speech consisted mostly of tweets and chirps, but it was easily processed and

2

decoded by the translator. There were no immediate covert threats or plots against us, unless the birdman in the corner had mistaken us for the "Tootbrained Threeshsweeper who left his sister on her nest" and would be receiving a well-deserved thrashing later that evening. Still, it paid to be careful, especially on a planet where technology was forbidden, mob justice was a fact of life, and aliens were regarded as intruders and regularly lynched. And humans, considered the worst of aliens, were treated even worse.

Despite my initial misgivings, the Shoorulians were proving easy to fool. Their tech sweeps were primitive and passed by the cybernetic enhancements, hidden weapons, and moebic mutants which were prevalent among our gear. Even the gravbelts passed right through. Still, I let Stosh guide me blind through the cone shaped buildings to this rendezvous without engaging my sight. I needed the sonar practice, and besides, the protes needed the time to propagate.

Wwwhhhrrr!!

I could sense the light now, but I still kept my eyes closed. I was already aware of the movement of bodies around me. The subcon trackers marked and catalogued each occupant. I scarcely paid them any attention. My quarry had not yet arrived.

Stosh sat quietly next to me. I could sense his wariness but on the motion detector he was practically invisible.

"You in?" he asked.

"Coming on line now".

I embraced the formless, pulsating colors for a last comforting moment... and then I opened my eyes.

sSSShhhhreeeeeessshhh-KKKTT

A million points of pain bombarded my retina. I

shook with torment as my eyes shredded with agony. My head imploded, my skull shattered, my eyeballs burst. I pleaded to God to end my suffering, but there could be no God who would allow the torture I went through.

I wanted to cry, but I couldn't. Tears were too dangerous to the beasties, so The White Coats took that function away.

It was over in a blink.

Outwardly, I showed nothing or maybe the slightest curling back of my lips. A smile or a snarl – take your pick. The White Coats promised that there would be no pain, but I'd like to put them through that just once.

Finally, I could "see".

Whhrrr

There was a rush of images – all different wavelengths, all different messages for the proc amps to sort through. I selected visual wavelengths for a starter and narrowed my vision to human scope – about 130 degrees. The proper lenses clicked into place, and I had my first view of a living Shoorulian.

There were certainly uglier creatures in the universe, but none of them walked on two legs – in fact, none even have legs. I learned with my new eyes, though, that beauty is in the eye of the beholder. I'm sure that Shoorulians must have thought that there is nothing so splendiferous as a mottled grey complexion, feathered outcroppings of blue down, and splotched orange beaks, but something about that thought was too disturbing, so I switched quickly to heat-scan which was less visually judgmental. Then, the natives – I kept forgetting that I was the alien there – appeared as greenish blobs casting blue after-images every time

4

they moved. It also allowed me to spot a number of illegal weapons with hot power sources burning in several tavern-patrons' pockets.

My implanted mechanisms were both hi-tech and lo-tech, very old and very new. And very experimental. All compact, and all implanted. Ranging from the sonar, radar, and laser enhancements to isotopic reactors, olfactory analyzers, and gene-spliced circuitry, all tied together by a computer which fit in a hollowed out wisdom tooth – which was where the White Coats had planted it.

But it was all nothing compared to the gift of sight.

I was born blind. My eyes were useless. They never connected to my optical nerves. Even with all the sci-tech leaps, it was impossible to make the neural connection to enable me to see. At least no one bothered to try. Until they needed me.

I never complained. I enjoyed belonging to a close community. A community of others like me. Not invalids, but a space-faring generation that travelled between the distant worlds and suffered the worst of relativistic implications (Einstein is not popular with my lot). Although others of my kind were handicapped, the inevitable result of close pre- and post- partum exposure to radioactive sources – the nuclear furnaces that make up the stars in our galaxy – our lives were similar in more important ways. My people were Orphans: Generation Two.

My life was provided for. I was given proximity sensors, motion detectors, level simulators – some were even implanted. I was more able and capable than many of my compatriots. I missed my father more than my eyes. That was a naive mistake.

My father was an Orphan: Generation One. It was never explained to me why he was allowed to procreate, or why I was placed in the next generation. I could only speculate. He must've been owed a favor.

They came to me one day. They offered sight and a chance to cross Generations. I turned them down.

They promised riches and adventure and fame. They didn't interest me.

They upped the ante. I would be given my own starship. A free pass to forbidden zones. Gation maps to wondrous places.

Again, I turned them down.

Then they made an offer I couldn't refuse – a chance to meet my father.

I accepted and found myself with the worst end of the bargain.

They fixed my eyes. The technology was ancient, but the application was new. It was based on amoebic-electronics, the use of bacteria, amoebas, and the tiny electronic fields they produce when confronted with certain stimuli. The White Coats gene spliced the little buggers to respond to particular stimuli in a predetermined way. Before dying an untimely death, the bacts produced enzymes that would pass through a neural interchange. The proteins signaled a human brain that its eyes saw electromagnetic flux, or a gamma ray emission, or a splash of reflected light. All those little creatures dying so that I may see. *Amazing grace!*

The therapy was quick and efficient. It was hardly painless.

The White Coats implanted the germs of sight. The quacks then said, "be fruitful and multiply". They did, and the bacteria to which I owed my sight – and

6

my life – nearly killed me.

The little bastards.

They spread uncontrolled beyond the safety zones set by The White Coats. They were an infection within my body. My immune system, even artificially augmented, couldn't keep up. Drastic steps were taken. I was filled with drugs. I was suspended in a bath of Gammaglucide. My body was frozen and thawed and frozen again, but even cryogenic therapy didn't work. It was the Old Man himself who stepped in and saved my life. He introduced a supplemental bacteria. One programmed to contain its fellows to a pool behind my pupils. My immune system recovered and fought back. Then, the genetically engineered mutants lived happily, multiplying and dying and dropping proteins and enzymes for the benefit of my sight – as long as they stayed behind the line. And my body was reinfused with super-mutant white killer cells and super-recovery/rebuilding genes. The White Coats said that I might be immortal. Or I might die prematurely when the killer cells evolve and cannibalize my body's vital systems. The debate continued, but in the meantime, I was put to work.

Every once in awhile, though, I wondered if maybe a few of the beasties escaped. Perhaps they were meant to.

Stosh had selected a table in the back with a view of the entire room. This was standard procedure for covert surveillance. It also meant that we were effectively surrounded by a couple of dozen hostile life forms. Stosh must have sensed my anxiety.

"Fair fight," he said as he sized up the room.

I had to agree. He hadn't seen the weapons blazing

within reach of the hostiles, but he could usually sense them and would assume that they were there. He did know about the weapons and armor we carried. We each had a laz tucked between the middle and index finger of each hand that could cut through a Shoorulian as easily as it cut through titanium. Our particle shields could stop all but the most sophisticated weapons, and our gravbelts brought a new dimension to hand-to-hand fighting. As a last resort, we each had a high-explosive kamikaze device implanted in our sternums. There was little here that could threaten us. Still, it didn't pay to underestimate the enemy. We gave the Shoorulians a healthy degree of respect.

There was a brief disturbance at the door, followed by the entrance of an entourage of bodyguards. They spotted us immediately, but only kept a wary watch on us as they cleared a path to a table near the bar. In the center of the group was an albino Shoorulian, apparently their leader. Probably the buyer. Not a true albino, either. I could detect chemical traces by which he came his light skin and feather color. A show-off. His guards were packing some heavy-duty heat, too. I sensed some cold-power among their possessions, too. Not a good sign for us. The balance of power may have swung in their favor. Still, as long as the other patrons minded their own business, then we would probably be okay.

I tried to sense "the item", but it either hadn't been brought in yet or it was well shielded. We had time, so we sipped our grog and waited.

My concentration was devoted to a deepsight, multi-layer analysis of the new group of Shoorulians, so I missed the entrance of the newest patron into the bar. But Stosh gasped slightly into his drink, for him a reaction akin to a point and a shout. Being directed toward us by the barkeep was a human. This would certainly bring us undue attention. There were few humans on this planet, and we were unliked, if not unwelcome. A gathering of more than a pair is considered a threat by the Shoorulians. The new human occupant turned and was walking our way.

Damn it! If "the item" were out in the open, we would have made our move and gotten out before the stranger got too close.

"Kit, is that your dad?" Stosh inquired. "He looks like you!"

I rarely used my beasty sight to look in a mirror, but I could see what Stosh meant. The man walking toward us was quite a few standard years older than myself, but there was an uncanny resemblance. The likeness was more like a father's than an uncle's. This was not a coincidence. And the timing could not be worse.

"No, my father is much younger. Even younger than we are."

Stosh gave a quick, curt nod of understanding.

He stood before us, blocking our view of the suspicious Shoorulians. I shifted and tried to dismiss the gentleman, but he persisted.

"Dad, it's me. Your son."

I shook my head but didn't turn. The Shoorulians were starting to get nervous. I wasn't sure I heard him right.

"You're mistaken, Gramps. I don't have a son."

"My name is Claude, and you are my father. I can prove it. Look at me!"

I looked finally. Genetic tests could prove it, but I trusted my sight. This man was related to me somehow, but my son? Obviously, this would demand my attention, but I had none to give at that moment. I pushed Claude aside, and he fell into a chair to my right.

Stosh sensed the glut of humans and stood. He backed away, in the direction of the watchful Shoorulian party. His eyes spoke volumes as he inched away from us. Things were coming to a head, and we were vulnerable.

"I don't care who you are," I tried to smile for those watching. I doubt if it was fooling anyone. "This is not the time." I looked around at the birdfolk who seemed to be closing in around us, "And definitely not the place."

"This is important," he said.

"I'm sorry, but I can't help you."

"It's not me. It's Mom. She's in trouble."

So were we. The door was still swinging from the latest human to enter the room. Of course, he made a beeline for our table. I knew this man who was about ten years younger than myself. My father.

Not the best time for a family reunion.

Stosh was still backing nonchalantly toward the Shoorulians. I could see power flare in the palm of his hand. He had kicked the safety off his laz.

Dad pushed past a couple of alien patrons and came directly to our table.

"The Old Man sent me. Your son is trying to find you. You are to 'avoid contact at all cost'." He spotted Claude sitting next to me. "Oops!"

"You're too late."

"That's bad."

"You have no idea."

The door was swinging again. I almost missed it,

but I wouldn't have missed the signature of the particle shield that came through the door. It was emanating from a backpack carried by a dark-cloaked human female with a single Shoorulian bodyguard. Beneath the shield was a barely detectable cold power source. This was "the item" we were sent to intercept. The woman carrying it approached the White Shoorulian without hesitation.

"So this is my Grandson?" Dad inquired with a chuckle. "Call me, Zachary. 'Grandpa' would be a little uncomfortable."

"Get out, now. There's trouble!" I barked pushing away from the table. "You know the drill, Dad."

He must've understood the tone in my voice, because he didn't hesitate in dragging Claude out of his seat and toward the door. Stosh's fingers glowed with full power.

Too late. The human spy was made aware of our party and knew immediately the threat that we posed. She whistled a quick order and the room around us seemed to move.

I kicked off my laz's safety switch. Time to go to work.

Stosh, who had been trying unsuccessfully to be inconspicuous, took several shots in the back. His shield protected him from the low power and percussion shots. The cold shots took the shield down a little, but it held. He turned and pointed two fingers at the woman, as if he was making an accusation, then fired a single laz shot which pierced the human's chest. She should have used her shield to protect herself instead of "the item". Stosh then turned his weapon on the nearest Shoorulian and sliced it in half.

Stosh took a lot of fire then, and his shield began to

11

waver. I jumped on the table to draw fire and get a bead on the backpack, which was easy thanks to the beasties behind my eyes. I fired a sustained burst that was absorbed by the shield surrounding it. It generally takes about thirty seconds with a laz to reduce a shield to nothing and get at the thing it protects. I wished again for the phase-wave weapon The Old Man promised us years ago.

I hit it for a solid twelve seconds before I was dragged down by a birdman. I was able to throw the light alien off me before he had the chance to tighten his claws around my neck.

Stosh fired on the item for another five. I sliced a couple of birds who tried to claw him down. Then they used Stosh as a shield, actually pulling him over the backpack and making it impossible to hit "the item" without cutting my partner apart. I leapt forward to get a better angle but was pulled down by a Shoorulian again. I couldn't break loose, and I couldn't get an angle to cut the creature off me.

I pushed another step to the weak center of the floor. It was easy to drag the hollow-boned Shoorulian, but their claw like grips were almost unbreakable. He made a leap at my throat as I dialed the gravbelt all the way up.

In effect, I had increased my weight a hundred times. The unstable floor gave way, and we plummeted into the deep basement. This was just like g-games at the Orphanage. I dialed the belt the other way for a perfect "touchdown" and sprang back up through the hole, encountering debris still falling from the bar and leaving the Shoorulian below.

I was hoping to find Stosh in a better state than I left him, but as I stepped lightly back up through the chasm, I saw him fighting desperately to pull away from the Shoorulians. I concentrated another blast at one his opponents. He was able pull himself away for another shot at the backpack. The shield was almost gone, but so was Stosh's. Another blast on him and Stosh was a goner. I started toward him, firing at the cowering aliens. I saw one of them aim weapon at him.

I wasn't going to make it.

I blasted a quick shot and the Shoorulian misfired, but there were others to take his place. There was nothing I could do, but I kept running toward Stosh anyway, belt set at low g. I pointed shots at everything that moved, but it was hopeless.

"Alpha...." I heard Stosh growl through gritted teeth. He stared hard at me as he sprawled across "the item".

He said it for my benefit. A warning.

It was the first of a series of keywords that would ignite the kamikaze device.

The message sank in immediately, but I kept going, hoping against hope that I could keep the aliens away from him. Save my partner somehow.

"...Omega...," Stosh screamed the countdown sequence.

My feet stopped; braked with aid of the gravbelt. Several hot shots blasted short, sparing the waning power on my shield.

But in my mind, I was still in the middle of it, slicing the Shoorulians to bits and saving Stosh. My special sight told me that his shield just failed. *Damn it, Stosh. Damn it!*

"...Infinity...."

A percussion shot hit me in the back. My shield held. I dialed the belt back to low g and pushed off toward the door. There was nothing I could do now. I was in midair, at the mercy of forces beyond my control – momentum, gravity, Stosh's timing. I hoped the explosion would propel me through the door to the relative safety beyond.

Stosh's last word: "...Amen...."

I felt the explosion as I hurtled forward, my ears deafened immediately by the crash. *Damn it, Stosh!*

"The item", a dozen Shoorulians and the best partner a blind spaceman could wish for disappeared in a cloud of brown dust as I tumbled into the street.

I lay there for a moment, hoping that this was just a dream. I stood and looked around for my father and son. They were nowhere to be seen. As nonchalantly as I could, I walked away from the burning building. I probably attracted more attention trying to appear calm than if I'd run in a panic but training had kicked in. The gathering Shoorulians, always looking for a reason to persecute a stranger, found me as a likely scapegoat. I called my personal transport and quickened my pace.

A few seconds later, the coffin-shaped vehicle dropped to my location. Just ahead of the mob, I stepped into the space vessel. I ordered it to lift-off as the birdmen began to thump on the sides of the transport. We rose quickly into a tight orbit of the planet. I ordered the ship to the nearest Orphan enclave.

"Assignment of navigational course contingent upon notification of mission status," responded the computer to my command.

"Let's go!" I screamed.

"Assignment of navigational course contingent upon notification of mission status," it restated calmly in my ear.

"Report to Orphan command: – " I growled as I thought back to the carnage and the loss of my partner. "'– Mission accomplished.'"

Chapter Two

I had Claude by the throat and pointed the laz at the orbital region of his skull. This was not going to be the run-of-the-mill father/son discussion.

I was not happy. The mission would have been an easy one if not for the untimely entrance of my father and son. We'd have stopped the exchange, and my partner would still be alive.

But I couldn't get myself to kick off the safety of my weapon. I needed too many answers, I told myself, but there may have been something else.

Dad seemed to sense that my resolve was wavering. He leaned against the ship's wall and just smiled.

"Okay," I hissed through clenched teeth. "Let's talk."

I could sense that Claude was strong, despite his age, but he offered no resistance. He just shrugged.

After the explosion, we used our personal transports to leave Shoorulia and rendezvous aboard an Orphan transport that was about to depart the system. Claude and Zachary were waiting for me. As soon as the door closed to Claude's quarters, I grabbed him. Dad made no move to stop me.

So here we were.

"Let's start with who sent you? No one was supposed to know I was on Shoorulia."

"It was The Old Man," Claude said.

"What? That makes no sense. Explain."

"Listen to him," said Dad. "And by the way, put your reeking fingers down before you create a generation gap between the lobes of his brain."

I pushed Claude away. He hissed a quiet sigh as he dropped himself into a chaise just out of my reach.

"It was our Old Man, not your Old Man. He oversees the human colonies. It seemed important that I find you, and The Old Men are the only ones in the universe who know what's happening between the Orphans and the colonies and the rest of the galaxy."

"But he must've known that sending you to Shoorulia would damage our mission!"

Strangely, it was Dad who was remaining calm in this situation. I'd never known that side of him before.

"Think about it," said Dad. "It might be the same person governing the different factions, but he probably has different objectives."

I bit my lip hard. It made sense. In my numerous dealings with The Old Man, he always seemed to have a hidden agenda. Confronting himself whenever he wants to expand Human Interest must be a daunting challenge.

"I'm sorry about your partner," said my son. "I wouldn't have wanted this to happen for anything. I would gladly trade places with him if I could."

"That may still be arranged," I snapped at him.

"Seems to me, Son, like you are getting angry at the wrong person. We didn't want this to happen. Get mad at the reeking Shoorulians who shot him down. Or at The Old Man who set things in motion."

Claude puzzled over his Grandfather's observation. "I'm still trying to fathom The Old Man. I don't understand him or how he runs things."

"I was there in the beginning," said Zachary, "And I still don't get it. Remember that there are more than one of him – seven, I think at last count – and they don't get along very well."

"What?" Claude asked incredulously.

"He's been cloned several times. Every time we need a new ruler."

"And they don't get along?"

"Think about it. Say there are seven of you. And each of you has a particular objective, none of which are compatible. One of you wants to create more colonies; one of you wants to stabilize the worlds where humans have already settled; one of you wants to provide trade and commerce between all worlds, human and otherwise. And you have to argue with yourself to get what you want, but the whole time, you know the arguments and the tactics you are most likely to use against yourself and so you have to come up with new arguments and new tactics."

"I'd go nuts."

"Exactly. And in the end, you commit some unthinkable acts of subterfuge to get your way. Like endangering his own agent's lives."

"But why would the colonial 'Old Man' want to disrupt Kit's mission on Shoorulia?"

"We may never know, but it's my guess that he wanted to drive a wedge between the few tenuous ties that Humanity has with the carping Shoorulians."

"An alliance with the Kozarians!" said Claude. "It would never happen while humans were on speaking terms with Shoorulia. We've been trying for years to bring the Kozarians to the table."

"Perhaps."

"So the Generation Two: Old Man told the Colonial: Old Man that Kit was on a mission to Shoorulia –"

"He'd have to get approval from the Council for any covert operations on an alien world."

"– And Colonial: Old Man sent me to find Kit, knowing that it would ultimately disrupt relations between Humans and Shoorulians. But how did he know that I would be looking for Kit?"

"He probably didn't. He just saw an opportunity and took it. Shad," swore Zachary, "If it wasn't this incident, then it would have been another. Maybe not for ten years or a hundred, but he would have found a way to accomplish the same thing eventually. My guess is that it worked, too. I'll bet that Shoorulia is breaking diplomatic relations with Humans even as we speak."

Zachary was right. We were all pawns in The Old Man's game. To be played whenever and wherever he saw fit. I wondered if Stosh saw any of this coming?

I took over the inquiry again. "Which brings us to our next question. Why were you looking for me?"

"Mom is in trouble."

"Ah. Questions. So many questions. Who exactly is 'Mom'?"

"Mom was a colonist on *The Carthaginian* –"

"My first ship."

"It was during The Last Evacuation from Earth. My mother's name is Trace Daruma. She was put into stasis a virgin and was pregnant when she awoke."

Zachary nearly fell over laughing. "My son! I

always knew you'd find a nice girl! Now, was she awake when you swived her or did she sleep through it all?"

"Yes. The ship's logs are a bit confused. Things don't quite jibe. Perhaps you could clear up the details?" Claude asked.

I could feel the tables rotating. Claude shot an accusing look in my direction. My father could barely contain his laughing. Maybe I should've lazzed 'em both and been done with it. I didn't like a lot of ties, which is one of the reasons I didn't get along with Dad. And I didn't like answering a lot of questions.

"So, tell me about Mom. Do you even remember her?"

I would never forget her.

The trip was to be a long one. Most of the habitable worlds close to Earth were already colonized. Many chose to live in biospheres orbiting the sun. The remaining population could only guess from astronomer's observations which worlds could possibly sustain human life. At that point, there had been few encounters with intelligent alien life forms. The only thing known for sure was that the colonial excursion would be long and the destination unknown.

But Earth was dying. Humans had depleted, destroyed, or consumed nearly every resource, and the planet could no longer sustain life. Every ship that could hold a person was loaded up, allocated scarce supplies and blasted toward a promising planet orbiting a distant star.

The Old Man oversaw it all. At the time, he only controlled a couple generations of Orphans. His compassion seemed endless at this time as he routed rare resources from distant points in the galaxy to accommodate the poor colonists. At the time, it seemed he wanted to give every living human a chance for a better life, but in retrospect, he was probably already looking to expand his influence to control the colonies.

At any rate, I had just been given my new sight. My first assignment was to be a fairly simple one: pilot *The Carthaginian* to the planet Bogolich. ETA was 240 years after departure. The ship had a sophisticated autopilot, so I was placed in a cryochamber along with the colonists. If there were no problems, I would be revived just a few days before the passengers to guide the craft into the atmosphere of their new home.

But there was a problem.

Life seeps back into you slowly when you come out of cryo. I was washed in an incubation gel and then the stasis capsule began to slowly vibrate to urge the blood to begin to flow. It doesn't always work. Of the thousand or so colonists, I knew already that about fifty could never be revived. I felt warmth begin to penetrate the gel and wash over my naked body and slowly, I began to move. If I'd had eyes, then I would have been greeted with a bright welcoming light. As it was, I let the beasties sleep for a little while longer.

"Emergency," stated a calm, mechanical voice. I could have chosen any number of voices for the ship's computer, but all of the human intonations gave me the willies, so I had dialed back the voice box to its most primitive mode before we even left Earth.

I pulled myself into a seated position. There was little g, so the effort was minimal. The surroundings were unfamiliar, though and so I spent a few minutes groping around the capsules. I remembered then to turn on my sonar. With this navigational aid, I easily found my way to the control couch.

"Emergency," rang the voice again.

"Is this a critical emergency, an urgent emergency, or just an emergency?" I asked. Suddenly, the question seemed to be ridiculous, but when you are traveling through the void of interstellar space, there are very few emergencies that are not spotted days or sometimes months before they have to be dealt with. I once performed an "urgent" maneuver in instell that required four manual adjustments to thrusters - each days apart with a margin for error of about four hours each. Anyway, the computer understood the question.

"This is a navigational emergency which must be corrected within thirty-seven hours and twenty-two minutes. Corrective action has already been undertaken and must be verified and approved within the critical period."

"Great. Get me some coffee, so I can 'approve' the corrective action and get back to bed."

"Pilot must be informed of the parameters of the corrective –"

"Is this 'critical' information, 'urgent' information or just 'emergency' information?"

"Corrective action is to be considered 'emergency information'".

"Only?"

"Only."

"Very good. Please don't mention it again until it is an urgent emergency, okay?"

"Instructions regarding classification and response of emergency is verified and implemented."

"Thank you."

"You are welcome."

"Help me. I'm scared."

I nearly jumped out of my skin. The soft, musical voice seemed to come from nowhere. I thought at first that perhaps the computer had reset its own voice box, but that just wasn't possible. I had lost track of the sonar scan – really wasn't paying attention to it – so I had no idea of the source.

I activated my seeing-eye bugs and was overwhelmed with the sensations that were still new to me then.

ZZKKTTT-WWHRRR!!!

A din filled the cavern behind my artificial eyes. A contrast to the sweet, lilting voice that startled me. Grinding, wheezing, crying. Crying? No, that was coming from the narrow passage leading to the bridge. The voice was sobbing now. *What the hell was going on?*

Zzkktt-whhrrr!

I saw spots, although I hadn't opened my eyelids. I tried, though, but my lids didn't respond. It wasn't happening fast enough. I saw each pixel as they burst – *hurry up!* –like an old stop-action vid of a flower – *Damn it! Get on with it!* – blossoming to life accompanied by a tiny poof – *Faster!* – and the acrid smell of burning sulfur – *No. I smelled honeysuckle. Sweet, yet pungent. No time for that! Pay attention. Get on with it, you reeking beasties!*

zzzkkkktttt -

My sight awakened, but I kept my eyes closed. No, I tried to tear them OPEN! My proximity sensors and auditory reactors gave me the details of the ship, but I missed something very important. Or something important had just happened.

"Emergency?" You can say that again!
wwwhhhrrr!!

I could sense the light, and I finally forced my eyes to open.

sSSShhhhreeeeeeessshhh-KKKTT

A million points of pain bombarded my retina – *FINALLY!*. I shook with torment as my eyes shredded with agony – *AT LAST!* My head imploded, my skull shattered, my eyeballs burst – *IT FELT WONDERFUL!* It was over in a blink.

Finally, I could "see".

whhrrr

It took a moment to focus. My panicked gaze met a vision of forlorn loveliness. Large, desperate eyes of a beautiful, young woman. She was free of clothing, her breasts perched like teardrops beneath soft shoulders and a gentle mist clung to her like an aura. Her hair drifted slightly in the low g. She held her arms out to me – an invitation or a request, but I didn't move.

The sad stare was full of curiosity and longing. I was confused and enticed and began to feel aroused. She noticed. I automatically switched my vision to heat sensors and discovered that her warm blood was responding to me, warming her lips, her cheeks, her breasts, her groin. I quickly switched back to normal vision before I became too analytical. I was not feeling very scientific.

She leaned – perhaps fell into me. Or perhaps I fell into her. Our arms and legs wrapped around us. Our lips met, and we gasped to breathe the same air. Her nipples were like spears, piercing my side. Soon I was piercing her, too. She gasped. Or perhaps it was me.

We made love as if we were the only humans in the universe, and at that particular place and time, we were. We thought it would never end.

It was love at first sight, after all.

It was days after we met, but we eventually succumbed to formalities. We introduced ourselves.

She was Trace Daruma. About my age. Perhaps a little younger. She was leaving Earth. Her family giving up on the planet after making a valiant and desperate attempt to find some way to survive. There was nothing there any more but death. She was betrothed to another colonist, Neville Bevington, but it was a formal arrangement. She had never met the man.

She confessed her love for me. I reluctantly did the same.

I wasn't reluctant because I didn't feel totally absorbed with this angel, but because I knew of this phenomenon. It was called "stasis obsession". It was an effect of being revived from cryo. It was said that it was like leaving the womb. It left the being in a state of emotional need after prolonged period of total dependence. The effect was well documented. In fact, crowds were known to form around cryogenic stasis chambers, waiting to capture an emerging person who would love them totally. At least for a while.

But it was still love, and I felt it as much as anyone ever has. So, I didn't share my suspicions about the true nature of our feelings with my lover.

"So you are the pilot of *The Carthaginian*?"

"Yes, my precious."

"That must be an important job, my sweet."

"Most everything is handled in autopilot. Except the landing. That's really the only tough part."

"You aren't watching over things during the voyage?"

"If I did, you'd find nothing but a chair full of bones when you arrived."

"Perhaps your child will take over the job for you."
Where did that come from?

"It would take several generations of Shickers to pilot this journey."

"Is that your last name then? Shicker? Where did it come from?"

"My imagination. I didn't like my Dad's name, so I made up one of my own. You can do that if you're an Orphan."

"Such a lovely name, too." She punctuated the thought with a suspended, warm kiss.

"It's a joke."

"Excuse me?"

"The name is a joke. I –".

She closed my mouth with another long kiss. We never did finish the conversation.

"Have you always been blind?"

"I'm not always blind."

"I mean were you born without sight?"

"Yes, but by the grace of The Old Man, now I can see."

"He is a wonderful person. He stocked most of this ship for us. Otherwise we'd have nothing. There was nothing left where we came from. Nothing but a few 'essentials'."

"I know. Perhaps we should break into the supplies for a few stitches of clothing."

A quick touch demonstrated that she appreciated our nakedness.

"I suppose the colonial supplies ARE off limits."

A passionate round of celebration followed the decision. Afterwards she became contemplative.

"Why was I removed from stasis?"

"I don't know. Computer error, I suppose. Cross circuiting when I was awakened. Something like that."

"Will I have to go back?"

"No. Never."

She drowsed in my arms. I thought this must be paradise. I also knew it wouldn't last.

A sense of urgency awakened me. I turned off the artificial gravity before we slept, so I was disoriented at first. Sonar helped. I didn't bother the bugs. They needed to replenish themselves after being worked hard for the last couple of days. And they were starting to give me headaches.

I found my way to the tiny bridge and pulled myself into the control couch.

"Where are we?" I asked the computer.

It rattled off a series of coordinates and referenced a map on the main control screen. I ignored the answer. I couldn't see the map, anyway.

"ETA?"

"Two Hundred Thirty-Seven years, One Hundred Twenty days, Standard Earth Years."

"Are we still in an emergency situation."

"We are approaching urgent emergency status – approximately two hours S.E.Y."

"I see." Motion detectors notified me that Trace was moving this way. I wanted to resolve this situation before she discovered that there was a problem.

"State nature of emergency."

"Inaccurate trajectory calculations based upon inaccurate mass allocation. Insufficient fuel to compensate trajectory with thrust rockets. Required dispersion of mass allotment to be fulfilled before re-ignition of compensatory thrusters for realignment of trajectory."

"I think I got that. Um, recommendations?"

"Corrective action has already been undertaken and must be verified and approved within the critical period."

"Define 'corrective action'."

"Nonessential mass has been catalogued for dispersal."

"Uhoh." I had a sudden, sinking feeling.

"And how much mass must be discarded before we fire the thrusters?"

"Fifty-point-nine kilograms."

"Hello, my love."

Trace was here. I was pleased with her presence. Not good timing, though.

"Trace, my darling. What is your, um, mass."

"We were weighed before we came aboard. I'm exactly fifty-point-nine kilograms. Why?"

"I think we have a problem."

We went through the manifest for hours, trying to find the " inaccurate mass allocation". Everything was in order, according to the records. The answer was a simple one.

"Smuggler."

"Smuggle what to whom?" Trace asked.

"Could be anything. The last few days of loading were hectic. Somebody hid something among the supplies. Doesn't have to be much. The fuel is allocated very precisely."

"I don't understand."

"It's very simple. The main engines are only used twice. Once for launch - to get the ship on the right course and to the right speed; next to decelerate and prepare to enter orbit."

She understood. "But the calculations were based on bad information."

"The discrepancies were enough to throw off the trajectory – not by much – but enough. After traveling at SuperEM speed for more than two years, we have a lot of space to cover. To correct our course now, we have to discard at least fifty-point-nine kilograms and use what little reserve fuel we have."

"Why me?" she cried. "Why not some of these things on the manifest?"

"Computer, why not discard some of the colonial supplies?"

"All supplies are classified essential for the establishment of the colony on the planet Bogolich."

"Is that so? Even the seven hundred kilos of gold? Or the thousand kilos of silver? The Orphans have found asteroids full of the stuff. What good is it for the colonists? Establish an economy based on pretty jewelry?"

"Gold is classified as essential for the establishment of the colony on the planet Bogolich. Silver is classified as essential for the establishment of the colony on the planet Bogolich."

"I see. What about junk food? There is a crate of chocolate on the manifest. Is that really considered essential?"

"All foodstuffs are classified as essential for the establishment of the colony on the planet Bogolich."

"What about these technical manuals? They are centuries out of date. 'Surviving In The Wilderness'? 'Life In The Wild'? Do you expect this will have any value on the planet Bogolich?"

"Technical manuals are classified as essential for

the establishment of the colony on the planet Bogolich."

"How about these other books? 'The Adventures Of Sherlock Holmes', 'Catch 22', 'Elephants In The Distance'. These people will be spending so much time surviving in the wilderness and building a new economy, when are they supposed to read this frivolous material?"

"'Frivolous material' is classified as essential for the establishment of the colony on the planet Bogolich."

"Okay. Is there anything on the manifest which is considered 'non-essential'?"

"Only essential items are allowed to be entered onto the manifest for transport to the colony on the planet Bogolich."

"I thought so. Is there anything on this ship which is halfway to 'the colony on the planet Bogolich' that is considered 'non-essential' to 'the colony on the planet Bogolich'?"

"Tolerable shrinkage of fifty percent pertaining to passengers is allowable before termination of destination and reclassification of colonists."

"And what is the current classification of said 'colonists'?"

"Colonists are redundant and classified as nonessential."

I turned to Trace. "That, my dear, is the crux of the problem."

"I don't understand. Why aren't colonists considered essential to the colony?"

"They are, up to fifty percent. It seems that there are just enough supplies for the colony to survive. Nothing that wasn't considered absolutely necessary was allowed in the hold. 'By whose judgment?' is a good question, but the fact remains that they stuffed the ship full of things they thought would be needed and then labeled it all as 'essential'. The computer can't touch it."

"But not the people?"

"Think about it. If the colonists were labeled as essential, then the ship would abort its journey if even one were lost enroute. We know already that we'll lose a few dozen coming out of cryo. If we want to keep the ship going to Bogolich, we have to allow for some 'shrinkage' of the colonists."

"So, I'm expendable."

"To the computer, yes, but not to me."

"So, what do we do now?"

"We do an inventory. We find the discrepancy in the manifest, and we correct it by dropping the contraband into instell." I stood and led the way back through the ship. The hold was sealed, and it took several minutes of arguing with the computer, finally utilizing priority override codes before the door slid open.

The hold was filled from floor to ceiling with pressurized cargo crates. Each was labeled with a numbered code that corresponded to an item on the manifest.

"What is current emergency status?"

"Urgent emergency status is now in effect. Critical emergency status will commence in four hours and must be resolved within eight hours S.E.Y."

"Okay, then. Let's start with 'a'. Computer, are 'aardvarks' labeled as essential for the establishment of the colony on the planet Bogolich?"

"There are no aardvarks listed on the manifest."

"Good, that's one less thing to look through."

Fortunately, we only had to look halfway through the c's before we found the contraband. Two crates of chocolate goodies were labeled with the same number. Much easier than stowing a 50 kilo crate behind a bulkhead and hoping that it wouldn't be noticed. It would have taken more forethought than I would have thought justified a satisfied sweet tooth. But chocolate was rare, even on Earth. And Earth's finer delicacies had a black-market value even then.

"Computer, verify item number 52312d423 as duplicate and reclassify."

"Duplicate number 52312d423 reclassified as redundant and unnecessary."

"Prepare to eject redundant item number 52312d423 and recalculate trajectory correction."

"Trajectory recalculated. Emergency. Thirty kilogram mass overage. Insufficient fuel. Recommend ejection of nonessential colonist number 432f."

Trace yelled, "What?!" There was a hint of panic in her voice.

"It's not enough. We can eject the original source of the problem, but we have to account for two years worth of being off-course." Trace still looked worried. She should know better than to think I would throw her overboard. And there was nothing the computer could do to force the issue, unless it blew the hatches and sucked us both into instell. I wondered if that was a course it might consider.

"Computer, recommend an alternate means to compensate for the mass overage."

There were a few tense moments of silence.

"Unable to compute alternative. Recommend ejection of nonessential colonist number 432f."

"What if we chucked the computer core into space?

Would that be enough to put us back on course?"

"Computer is considered essential for the establishment of the colony on the planet Bogolich." I didn't ask for an explanation, but it went on to list several hundred functions that it performed to keep the ship on course and the colonists alive. The computer was no dummy.

"Okay, if we put both crates of chocolate into instell, would that be enough?"

"Nonredundant item number 52312d423 is essen–"

"Theoretically?"

"Theoretically, the action you suggest would be sufficient to correct course and provide for greater margin of error."

"It would be more than enough?"

"Yes."

"If I gave you an override code, would you let me dump the original box o'chockies?"

"Loss of original item number 52312d423 would compromise the mission."

"That would be bad?" Trace inquired.

"Yes. That would be bad. It would put this flight at risk. Maybe our lives."

"So we are stuck back where we were."

"Not necessarily. We just have to convince the computer that the original chocolate has served its purpose. Then it can be ejected without a problem."

"So, we have to eat the chocolate?"

I unsealed the crate and opened a mylar envelope of candy.

"A traditional gift between lovers, I believe." I popped one in my mouth and offered one to Trace. "Sweets to the sweet."

It was easy to convince the computer that the functions of the foodstuffs were to sustain the crew and the colonists; therefore, we were allowed to consume it. We ejected the "redundant" crate and then went to work on the original one. We had the computer use the original crate as a disposal container and rerouted the waste from the sanfac into it. When we had the exact mass needed to make course corrections, then it would be dropped into space, and we'd resume our trip to Bogolich.

It took weeks to make it through the stacks of rich chocolate. At first, it was heaven. We made love and snacked on chocolate. Slept and snacked on chocolate. Snacked on chocolate and snacked on chocolate. But all good things come to an end. And as we gnawed our way through the end of the goodies, we realized that we would soon be at a decision point that would change our lives.

We split the last piece, used 'the facility' and checked the mass of the container. It was time to launch, meaning that we would detach the crate and use thrusters to push us onto a new course. We did so mutely, giving only a few brief commands to the autopilot.

Trace began the discussion, bravely facing facts that I was still trying to ignore.

"You can't live on Bogolich with me can you?"

I winced. She knew the rules. Orphans are restricted from fraternizing with the rest of humanity. It was for our own good. For their own good. We would become a jumbled, non-rooted, unstable society.

"I can't. I might be able to get you Orphan status. I'm owed a favor. My dad...."

She looked hopeful for a moment, then her face

went glum.   It was a tough life even if she was accepted, and she wanted to build a home on a new world.   I admired her spirit, but I didn't want to take away her dreams.

"No. It's not right. It's not what either of us want," Trace uttered glumly.

"So what do we do?"

"Let's go to bed."

Hours later, we were back in stasis, dreaming of our lost paradise.

And so, we were back on course.

"I didn't know she was pregnant, of course.   The first time I ever heard that I had a child was when you burst on the scene a few hours ago," I explained to my son.

I saw her reviving from stasis, and I left without saying goodbye. I was reassigned to a new ship and a new mission. I thought I'd forget her.

"Would it have made a difference?"

"Yes. No. I don't know. It's impossible to say. Would I have left the Orphans to raise a family? No. Definitely not. Maybe. Yes. Hypothetical situation, and I'm sorry, I can't give you an honest answer."

"Would you leave now to save her life?"

Trace, dear Trace.   I know why we fell in love before, and it wasn't just stasis obsession. *There was more to it than that. Ten years have gone by in my life. How many in yours? Do you still love me now? Could you still love me?*

Do I still love you?   YES!

"Yes."

Claude smiled at my answer. I looked at my son for the first time. His face was marked with many long years of struggle. Could I have made it easier for him if I'd settled on an alien world and raised him myself? Probably not. He had lived longer than me, and I couldn't have promised him an easier life. He could probably teach me a few things, and I didn't even know where he'd been or what he'd done. I wasn't sure that I'd have been a good father. God knows my father was not a good example to follow. Claude seemed to have made good on his own. If he'd had contact with The Old Man then he must be fairly important in his sector of the galaxy.

"Where is Trace, and what kind of trouble is she in?" I queried.

"I don't know. I've been trying to locate her for months. She wasn't on Leerelly when I tried to find her."

"Leerelly? Why was she on that reeking, forsaken planet?" asked Zachary.

Claude exhaled deeply. "Long story. I'll give you the short version - .

"We arrived on Bogolich to find that the planet was inhabited by Bogolichians. They were quite harmless, but we were not welcome. We spent several years there while we waited to find a new destination. We were finally granted settlement rights on Marmotley. We were told that it was uninhabited and an ideal planet for humans. Off we went. I was about seven years old, Standard Earth Years, at the time.

"I was curious about who my father was. The other colonists were curious, too, but Mom never said. I guess she was trying to protect you."

"Or herself."

"Maybe. Anyway, we went into stasis, again. But when we arrived, we found that there was a colony already there. Humans this time, and they weren't as friendly as the Bogolichians. This colony had beaten us to the planet and staked a claim before we reached there."

Zachary nodded. "Space-folding. Discovered about two hundred years ago, Standard Timeline. Sometimes three or four times as fast as SuperEM."

"We were considered refugees and not allowed to leave the ship. Our settlement claims were considered expired before we arrived and the new Marmotlians were granted the planet. Of course, it took about ten years to settle the claim and find a new planet to settle. I grew up on a station orbiting Marmotley, and tried to find out who my father was."

"So, then you left for Leerelly."

"Not yet. First we tried to settle on Slebster, in the Watre sector. We actually had the colony up and running for a few weeks before we discovered that there was another claim on the planet. It was finally agreed that we could share the planet. That was okay with about half the colonists, but the other half hopped back on board the ship with half the supplies and headed for Leerelly. Mom was one of them. I was tired of not having a home. And, I wanted to find out about my father. So, I stayed. I was even married for a while. I got a job in the colonial council and in my spare time I researched *The Carthaginian*. The ship's logs have been altered, by the way."

"My doing, I'm afraid."

"I suspected as much, although I think someone else has been in there, too."

"Oh? Why do think that?"

"Because somebody deleted the pilot's name, for one. I couldn't think of any reason you'd have to do

37

that."

Curious –, I thought. "I didn't. I just deleted the fact that Trace was brought out of stasis, and that we'd ejected some cargo."

"Well, there were bigger gaps in the information than just that. I only found you by checking the cryo manifest and comparing it to the colony roll call. Anyway, I figured something must've happened and you and mom.... well, then there was me."

"And so where is your mother?"

"I don't know. The ship folded into warp thirty years ago. When it reached Leerelly, mother wasn't on board."

"How is that possible?"

"I don't know. I saw her get on the ship myself. I saw the ship fold. But when it arrived, she was gone."

Zachary was puzzled. "Shad! Ships don't just fold and unfold in and out of warp – "

"I know, but I can't explain it."

"She's in trouble," I said, shaking my head.

"That's what I've been saying."

Chapter Three

I volunteered to discuss the situation with The Old Man. He wanted to see me anyway – a debriefing on the Shoorulia mission. I had some questions to ask him about that, too. I also had thoughts of resigning. Not the piloting part, but the Special Agent part. I was losing the stomach for it.

First, I needed to check-in with The White Coats. It was a tightly secured area of The Hub, but my retina scan was so unusual, that the door practically flew off the hinges.

The biotech arena was just past The Old Man's regen tanks. I considered turning on the beasties to scan the progress of the clones, but the bacts needed the rest. Walt could fill me in, anyway.

Walt met me at the door. He tried to take my arm and lead me in, but I pulled away too quickly. He still remembered me from before my basic installation.

He had me under the lights in a moment. Blood and other fluids were analyzed, reactions checked, and sensors calibrated, but he was most interested in the beasties. A microscopic scoop took a sample from a hidden shunt in what used to be a tear duct, and I was finished. The protes were then the focus of the examination.

"Low count on the infrared. Visual spectrum is a little scarce, too. To be expected. The others are low, too, but there weren't many of them implanted to begin with. Give 'em all bed rest and drink plenty of water. They should be back to optimum performance in no time."

"Thanks, Walt. How's The Old Man?"

"Another one dropped last week. We're keeping up, barely. We've started using alpha wave transmitters to keep the thoughts updated. The memory transfers weren't always taking."

The Old Man was the only being in the universe allowed, nay required, to clone. He was ancient, but by legal decree, he must be replaced with a functional clone in the event of death. Limited means were allowed to keep him alive and healthy, but the same law prohibited him from being given cybernetic implants. Too much power in one man's hands, I guess.

"We've got a dozen of 'em ready at any time, but half of those won't make the initial cut and half of the rest wouldn't last a week. We throw away more flesh here than the soldier farms."

"I'll check back in later. Keep The Old Man going."

"Losing battle, but we try."

I made my way back to the security door using only proximity sensors. Most of the cybernetic enhancements would be turned off before I could see The Old Man, anyway. Our tech scans here were much better than the Shoorulians and active enhancements made his bodyguards nervous. His conference chamber was as close to the center of the universe as existed for humankind, and it was carefully protected.

I dismissed the transport that came for me and walked the inner spiral toward the Generation Two Sanctum. As usual, there was traffic going both directions within The Hub. The Old Man had gadgets galore to bring in information, but he preferred to get his news from eyewitness sources. With space-folding transports available to him, no one was too far away to talk to. He made history everyday – in every timeline.

Humans discovered the first SuperEM transport late in the twenty-first century. It wasn't The Old Man who'd discovered it, but he was right in the middle of implementing it. It happened just in time, too. We were polluting and over-populating Earth, and we needed a way out. Leaving the planet seemed the only solution. So we started creating ships to evacuate humans.

The Old Man saw his chance to provide a useful service – and expand his power.

He realized that the people that would be piloting the spacecraft would need to get special treatment. Not only would they be facing danger but they would be far removed from the rest of humanity. The evacuees – excuse me – colonists would be living sedentary lifelines while the pilots would be subjected to the effects of relativity. Time would move more slowly for the pilots who travelled at the speed of light and faster – they would age minutes while their colonial counterpart aged years. In effect, the pilots would live in a different universe than the rest of Humanity.

And by controlling the pilots, The Old Man would control humanity.

That wasn't a necessarily a bad thing. The Old Man was a compassionate, kind, thoughtful, and intelligent person who knew when to be cold, calculating, ruthless, and cruel. He was a fitting ruler for a species of the same ilk.

He was elected to his first position simply because he was the only person smart enough to calculate the relative factors concerned in meshing a population which aged at different rates. If a pilot aged too quickly, The Old Man would assign her to a ship traveling faster than the speed of light. If he was aging too slowly, he would be assigned to a slow boat to Chinzeria.

At first, The Old Man took only orphans as pilots, but soon he found that he was creating a new, self-contained society. The spouses, sons, and daughters all belonged and indeed, were needed to make it work. Contact between Orphans and colonists was at first restricted and soon was forbidden – bonds between the two societies would soon be broken by the chasm of relativity and distressing relationships would result. My immediate family was a case in point.

The First Generation went well, but it wasn't enough. There weren't enough pilots to guide our ships to the far points in the galaxy. The returning pilots would have grown too old to be of use to their society, and their daughters and sons were too young to fill the void. So, the Old Man created a new Generation to fill the gaps. Generation Two. My Generation.

But there was only one Old Man, and he had his hands full shuffling First Generation pilots. So he was cloned in order to perform the same duties for Generation Two. In the meantime, colonial society was breaking down. Our species had spread too distant to be governed well, and the leadership council was too old to get a grip on it. The Old Man stepped in and made things right. Clone number Three.

Between the three of them, they controlled all humans spread halfway across the galaxy. Some say he had it planned all along.

Now, there were several Old Men and their continuity was due to a tenuous cloning technology. But it worked well enough – the Old Man still lived after countless centuries.

And he was the best source of information in the universe.

I met Clarice outside The Old Man's Sanctum. I turned on my sight once I shook her hand, but I kept it tuned to visual mode only.

She was an ageless woman with a permanent frown and perfume that smelled like old chalk. She tied her hair back so tight that it threatened to tear her skin at the temples. It was rumored that she and The Old Man were lovers, but I knew she was too old for him.

She scanned me for tech and put on her sourest pout. She found every implant and seemed upset by each one she discovered. I shrugged. She knew about them all anyway. She recommended half of them. She probably would not have let me past, but it was The Old Man who requested this meeting, and he got what he wanted.

The shield on the door phased momentarily before I was allowed entry. I heard it zip back into place once I passed the threshold. The Sanctum was the innermost ring of The Hub. The ring was cut into several sections - one for each Old Man. Beyond the ring of Sanctums was the Inner Sanctum where the Governing Council met. Of course, the Council was made up of only one person, but he was in attendance as all of the several members.

I was eyed by four of The Old Man's guards. They were all paraplegics, so I knew that they were loaded with cyber weapons. The law provided that invalids only could be enhanced with biomechanical tools. Thus, I received eyes thanks to my blindness; the guards owed their strong limbs to their disabilities.

I waited patiently for The Old Man to appear. I declined a seat. He rarely kept his sources waiting for long.

Within moments, he entered. There were shouts from an intense argument coming from the Inner Sanctum. The noise disappeared as the door sealed tightly behind The Old Man. He nodded in the direction of the door.

"Crazy. All of them," he laughed.

He hobbled in on a hickory cane, but otherwise looked in remarkably good shape for a centuries-old human. All of his hair was gone, including his eyebrows. Light reflected off his skin from active chemical disinfectants that killed germs on contact. His immune system was needed for more important things.

He chuckled heartily as he offered his hand. I ignored it. I was trying to make a point, after all.

He seemed genuinely disappointed by my lack of civility as he fell into a stiff chair. He took a sip from a bottle he unstrapped from his belt – medicine, I supposed.

"Kit," he said, "I heard that your mission went badly, but certainly," he reached out to me as if he knew nothing of my complaint, "I am not to blame."

"That's where you're wrong."

"No, Kit, no. I had nothing to do with it."

"My partner is dead."

"I know. Poor Stosh! He was a good agent. One

of my best. How did it happen?"

As if you didn't know! "We were compromised."

"Compromised? How? Somebody pointed you out as agents?"

"In a sense."

"'In a sense'? What 'sense'? Please explain exactly."

"We were identified by a human. You know the Shoorulians are suspicious of us. When four of us showed up together it blew our cover."

"Your father didn't reach the intruder in time? Oh dear. I sent him to stop the man."

"It just made things worse, and you knew it would!"

"You're saying that I deliberately sabotaged your mission to Shoorulia? My God, do you know what would have happened if they had gotten hold of 'the item'?"

"I don't even know what 'the item' was."

"Nor should you have known. Suffice it to say that it put all of Humanity at risk. Stosh was right to give his life to destroy it. He's a hero because of it. He saved Humanity."

"We could have destroyed it without losing anyone, if – "

"If what? There were factors at play there that you don't know about. I truly wanted to stop your son from interrupting the mission. I truly did. Yes, one of the council wanted to force an issue with the Shoorulians. He succeeded. That was not my goal."

"You are he."

"I was. My interests lie elsewhere, now."

"My son should have never been told where I was."

"Which raises another issue –" I wasn't through with the first issue, but there was no stopping The Old

45

Man. "Your son is a colonist – a rather important one, I gather. But how did he come to BE?"

"I think you are well familiar with the biological process," I said.

"You know the policy regarding contact between Orphans and colonists."

"I know the policy, not the penalty."

The Old Man grinned. "Actually, I thought we might discuss that."

"I've done enough. My debt had been paid in full. The Shoorulian experience evened the score as far as I'm concerned. I'm going to retire as Special Agent and pursue other interests."

"The score is NOT settled! You don't know how I've protected you and your family interests for centuries! Requests for family information from Marmotley to Leerelly, requests for flight information from *The Carthaginian*. There has been a good deal of interest in you, my boy. You're lucky you haven't been lynched."

"That's putting it a bit strongly."

"You'd be surprised. The point is that I'm not done with you yet."

"But I'm through with you."

"I expect your help on one more mission. Or else."

"Or else what? You'll kill me? Or set me up to be killed, like on Shoorulia? Go ahead! I like my freedom too much to live without it. So go ahead. Take your best shot!"

The Old Man stared hard at me for several seconds. Then his eyes softened.

"You're sly, Kit. You're learning, aren't you? Playing the game. Okay, I'll grant you that I still need you, but you need me, too. If you want to find your 'wife'."

I guess I never really intended to resign because my resolve faded when The Old Man mentioned my real reason for seeing him.

I approached the table at which he was seated. I tried to be tough, but it was hard to be forceful when he could see right through me. The guards sidled a little closer as I got nearer The Old Man.

"Okay," I said, "let's barter. You know where Trace is?"

"No, but I can find out."

"You're sure?"

"Of course."

"And what makes you think I won't find her on my own."

"Maybe you could, but there are complicating factors which I'm better equipped to handle."

"And what do you want from me?"

"Another mission. Not a complicated one. You wouldn't even lose much on your timeline."

"You make it sound so easy."

"Couldn't be simpler. I just need you to do what you do best."

"That is?"

"Watch. Observe. See. In your special way."

"Explain."

The Old Man actually cracked his knuckles before taking another swig from his medicine jar. He motioned impatiently for me to sit across from him at the table. I acquiesced.

"The unfortunate incident on Shoorulia has had repercussions to the Human Interest. The ruling faction on that planet was so upset about the destruction and mayhem caused by a few humans – I think that actually they were most upset by the loss of 'the item' – that they broke all relations with us."

"That's a terrible shame."

"Isn't it? Well, the happy consequence is that their mortal enemies, the Kozarians, are now willing to talk to us." *Claude was right.* "We've been trying to get the Kozarians to treat with us for a millennium. They don't trust us."

"I can't imagine why...."

" – And they control a quadrant of space which is vital to Human Interest." The surface of the table shimmered then disappeared to be replaced with a three dimensional representation of the galaxy. The Old Man put his hands in the middle of it as if he were about to rearrange the stars.

"You see, The Hub is here," he explained. "Human colonies are arranged all through this space, but Kozar is here, right in the middle. They have a number of planets ripe for human expansion, but they won't let us in."

"The bastards!" The Old Man ignored my sarcasm and continued.

"They haven't expanded themselves, because they have trouble at home. Their star is in a strange nova phase and is blinding their people. We've offered help, but they wouldn't even talk to us while we had relations with the Shoorulians."

"And now that has changed."

"Yes."

"And you want me to spy on the blind."

"Not exactly. They can see, now, thanks to some devices that they finally accepted from Humanity. It is similar to your implants, but simpler and self-contained in optical headgear. I invented it myself – in my spare

48

time."

"I see."

"Yes, you do. That is a good way to put it. In fact, you'll be the only human on Kozar who can see. The rest of the negotiating party will have retinal shields to protect their eyes. You'll be their guide."

"The blind leading the blind."

"And you will also be watching for anything unusual. You will be able to see their world as the Kozarians see it. It will be an important bit of intelligence and shouldn't require any covert acts of subterfuge."

"As simple as that?"

"Nothing more."

But I knew better.

Chapter Four

As a last second concession, I was able to convince The Old Man to give my son special dispensation – he would have special status as an Orphan: Generation Two. There would be much to teach Claude. I hoped that he would be a quick learner.

On leaving the Sanctum, I turned off visual mode and guided myself by proximity sensors. Walt said to give the beasties a rest, and I had a feeling that I'd be using them a lot in the near future. It meant leaving without seeing Clarice's smiling face, but that wasn't missing much. I felt like spending an evening in a safe haven, so I collected Claude and turned in the direction of the Orphanage on the outermost ring of the Hub. Zachary had already signed into the Generation One Orphanage. We agreed to meet in neutral territory in a few hours. I was hoping to give Claude a quick tour and then leave him to his own devices. I had much to discuss with my father and son, but I needed to spend some time with the folks I really considered family – my Generation.

There was a crowd assembled around the entrance to the Orphanage. It was almost a requirement to assemble and greet the returning Orphans at an appointed time every day.

There were five of us, including Claude and me, ready to step over the symbolic threshold. I knew the other three, but they weren't close friends. Still, we gripped and grinned like schoolmates. I didn't explain my connection to Claude, and the other Orphans politely declined to mention it.

"What happens next?" Claude asked.

"Brief ceremony, a few hugs and then people go back to their business."

"And they do this everyday?"

"Yes. Most people won't spend much time at the Orphanage, so it is an event for everyone, and it helps make everyone feel at home."

The door opened, and we mounted a platform that comprised the threshold into a large section of The Hub.

A voice I recognized from countless welcoming ceremonies enthusiastically announced, "Please welcome back from countless journeys and adventures, your own fellow members of Generation Two!" There was hardy applause as each of our names was announced. Claude received as much applause as the rest of us, even though no one in the crowd had heard of him before.

We dismounted the platform and went through the gauntlet of well-wishers. We were welcomed warmly. There were hugs and shouts and brief salutations exchanged throughout the crowd.

Claude was impressed. "Wow. I feel like I'm well-known, now. You do this for everyone?"

"Everyone is always welcomed back. People might spend years of their timeline away from the Orphanage. Some, like Stosh, never make it back."

Claude turned away, embarrassed. I put a comforting hand over his shoulder and continued the tour.

"This is where you grew up?" he asked.

"Yes. I consider the Orphanage my home. These are the people who taught me to live without sight. And later, taught me to live with sight. I owe many of them my life and some owe me theirs – not that any of us ever expect to be repaid."

"This is quite an arrangement," Claude said.

"The Orphan lifestyle is one of the few things The Old Man got right," I said.

We explored the outer edge of the Orphanage that was made up of shops of various kinds. None of the shops were staffed with sales personnel.

"I've never seen such a variety of goods? Where do they all come from?"

"Everywhere the Orphans travel. These shops are stocked by Orphans returning from various worlds. If an item is bought, the Orphan who supplied the goods will be credited. Overt capitalism is discouraged by The Old Man, which makes it all but illegal."

"But you could make a ton of credits selling this stuff in the colonies. Most of them produce such a specialized product that there are not a great variety of luxuries available. Some of this stuff is impossible to obtain!"

"I suppose most Orphans could retire on a colonial world with the spoils of their travels and would be considered wealthy, but earning a lucrative salary is discouraged, and frankly, it's downright unnecessary. Everything we need is provided by the Orphanage." I registered a pocketful of Shoorulian mollusk shells that I was glad to be rid of.

"Couldn't someone steal this stuff?"

"I suppose. They are welcome to it. If no one ever buys them, it's okay by me."

Claude ogled more of the shops' goods. I waited patiently for him as he plundered one shop of its entire store of crystal coral. He purchased it for more credits than I had on account and seemed pleased that he was getting "such a deal." He claimed it would make a great present to give to Trace on her return. I had still not discussed The Old Man's deal with him. Her return might be farther away than he imagined.

"How many Orphans are there?" Claude asked.

"My Generation? There were only a couple of thousand of us, and only about a third of our numbers are ever here at the Orphanage at any given time. The rest were on missions somewhere, sometime. I was reminded of a quick check that I had to make. "Speaking of given time...."

I logged onto a public com terminal, of which there were several around the Orphanage.

I explained, "I always make the effort to compare timelines. We have a Standard Time Calendar installed here that we can check against. The Old Man never fails. I'm always within a standard month or two of my age. Just to make sure, though, it's a good idea to check against friends' timelines."

We were making our way toward the housing combs on the inner side of the ring. I wanted Claude to get acquainted with our housing arrangements, but I had a personal mission, too. Stosh was a true orphan – no parents – but he did leave behind loved ones. I felt obliged to deliver the bad news myself.

I checked us into a double cube and left Claude to freshen up. My destination was just a few meters away.

I rang the outer com to her door. Delores answered equipped with a stoic, expressionless voice.

"We heard," was her simple answer. I was glad that I had decided to give my sight a rest.

"The Old Man said he was a 'hero' for humanity."

"Yes. That's what we were told."

"It's true. I'm sorry."

"Me, too. You're welcome to stay awhile, Kit. I've got a long stay over this time."

"Thanks, but there is some other important business I need to take care of. I leave in a couple of days."

"You're always welcome. Kit – I know you did what you could."

"I tried," I said, wishing that I could convince myself.

My "important business" was on the gravcourt. Claude was excited about seeing the sport that he had only heard about. His contact with gravbelts and their function were limited to low-g spacecraft and high-g planets. He had never seen one operated by a master.

He was impressed with his first sight of bodies bouncing around the inside of the clear vinlastic spheres. His intellect had resided for too long on natural gravitic worlds to make sense of bodies changing weight in midflight. He stopped in awe in the doorway, and I had to half-drag him inside.

Inside, we were greeted with the sound of distant echoing voices, shouting in thrill at a score or cursing a nearly illegal tackle. We encountered the odor of disinfectant mixed with human sweat that was familiar to anyone who had close contact with sport activities.

Claude balked at initiating himself on the

beginner's court and decided instead to watch from the stands. At first, I declined an offer to play gravball and instead bounded slowly around the edges of one of the spheres. Without visual cues, it was almost like sensory deprivation, which is what I desired, but my thoughts kept invading the voids that I was hoping would fill my mind.

I finally gave up and decided to join the game.

"Are you going to use your sight?" Claude asked. He was a little afraid for me. He knew that I'd been operating blind since I left The Old Man.

"Even blind, my enhancements give me an advantage. If I turn my sight on, it would just be too unfair."

"How is it played?"

I was double-checking my shield – the only safety equipment needed in the spheres. "Simple really. The object is to toss the ball into the circles at either side of the sphere and to prevent the other team from doing the same. No complicated rules – no need for them. I mean, you can try to hold someone on the other team, but he or she is liable to dial a high g-setting on you and crush you on their next bounce."

"Sounds dangerous –"

"It would be except that our shields protect us from the adverse effects of a heavy impact."

"Well, be careful!" he called as I entered the sphere.

I laughed, "Now who's sounding like a parent?"

I took the light point position and was matched against Sara Fulafs. She was practically a fixture in the sphere. We'd played on the same court many times in the past.

She checked me hard on the opening play. It jarred

me hard, but I found I needed it to get me started. I dialed high the next time she came for me and this time it was she who was stunned. I used the opportunity to push off and spring toward the goal. I grabbed a pass, but found that I had a bad angle for a shot, so I sprang in a path perpendicular to the circular opening that was our team's objective. Sara responded admirably, shielding me from the net, so I glided past her and faked the shot. As she slid by, I calculated a new trajectory and threw the ball hard into Sara's back. As planned, it caromed off her shield past the surprised goalie for the first point of the game.

"You reeking codfish!" she screamed at me. It was satisfying to see her competitive side.

Much of the rest of the game was the same. The physical activity was good for me. The release was what I needed.

After slamming home my fifth goal, I left the game with my team up seven to four. Not bad for a blind ballplayer.

"You were a little hard on Sara out there," observed Garret Kern, another old buddy who had been spectating and had struck up a conversation with Claude.

"It was nothing personal, only physical," I explained.

We returned to our modest cube. Equipped with Spartan accommodations, it fit my mood, but Claude was clearly uncomfortable in the rough lodgings. Still, he found sleep hours before I did. I found myself unable to close my eyes. I decided to do some research.

The Orphanage was always alive. The Old Man could age us the same, but he couldn't regulate our bioschedules. There were always some of us up and about. I sought out Pat Ondebeck from our cube's com terminal, and it pinpointed his location in the commissary. He was several years my senior, but we had spent time together as he trained me in the Orphan program. He was one of the first in our Generation. I had also learned from the old logs that he had been to Kozar many years ago.

"Hey, Kit! Married yet?"

"Not really."

"Find a nice gal?"

"Actually, I'm trying to find her now."

"Sounds good. How's the timeline?" I gave him my standard age. Pat had aged within a week of me on his timeline. The Old Man was amazing.

"I'm off to Kozar in a few days." It was no secret, but I hesitated slightly before revealing the information.

"Arrggh. Awful place. I guess you're the right person to send there. I mean, your eyes and all."

"I guess. Anything I should know?"

"I was there just before their sun went nova. Before you were even born. Tried to get the shadheads to talk with us, but no dice. They'd been duking it out with the Shoorulians, and they hated us for even talking with their enemy. It's not like we were supplying weapons or anything. They just had this 'friends of mine enemy' attitude that defied logic. But I guess we needed the route through Shoorulian territory, and there were no guarantees with the Kozarians."

"Did their sun show symptoms of going nova at the time?"

"No, but The Old Man must've suspected something, we did a quick survey, but there was nothing unusual about the star. Keep in mind; this is a strange kind of nova. It flares, sends out all sorts of

EM, blinds and burns, but never explodes. I think the nova feeds on itself. Could go anytime though, I guess. I don't envy you."

"Me, either. What about the people?"

"Basically humanoid, as you'd expect. Some could pass for humans. Some were really gorgeous, but I remember they had weird hair."

"Attitudes?"

"Ruthless bastards. Black and white, no grays. We don't have much info, but there is a file in the library. Download it before you go. Good way to pass time in instell."

"Thanks. I'm looking for a partner, by the way. I'm slated to fold in two days."

"Can't help you. I leave in a week for Betelgeuse. Long trip, and I hope they'll compensate the timelines right. Check the rolls?"

"I did. No one jumps out at me."

"Sorry. Someone will occur to you."

"I'm sure someone will –" A couple of people already had, but I was having a hard time coming to grips with the idea.

"No," Zachary stated bluntly.

"We won't do it," concurred Claude.

"You have no choice." I didn't. Why should they?

"I can't. If I'm to track down Mom, I've got to be in The Hub to look through records."

Zachary objected, "And I don't want my carping timeline mixed up with yours any longer. Things are confused enough as it is."

"Look. You got me mixed up in this, and I need a partner. Neither of you alone will do, but maybe together –." I was still operating without sight, so I

58

couldn't read their expressions, but I could sense from their shifting movements that they were searching for a way out. I had some leverage to apply.

"The Old Man seems to think this is important. He'll owe us a favor."

"Did he know where Mom was?"

"He said he didn't, but I think he does. At any rate, if he doesn't know then he can find out. But he won't until the Kozarians are in line."

"He just wants you there to 'observe'?"

"There's more to it than that."

"Carp it all!" Zachary cussed. "You know he wants someone close to the reeking Kozarians in case things get dicey."

"Or in case he needs someone to control them," I said.

"Or worse," said Zachary.

Claude knew what his grandfather meant. The comment was met with silence. Zachary was thinking of one of the more ominous reputed functions of the Orphans. Assassination.

I'd killed before, but not on order and never in cold blood. And only when circumstances warranted the action. I was afraid that I was being positioned to commit this crime, but The Old Man should have known me well enough to realize that I'd balk at the command.

"I need partners I can trust to keep me out of the 'worse' scenarios," I finally said.

"He wouldn't ask that –," Claude looked from me to Zachary. "Would he?"

"If it served Humanity's purpose...."

"Wouldn't that start an interstellar war? If the Kozarians are so belligerent and our assassination were discovered - "

I shook my head. "Don't be ridiculous. There will never be an interstellar war. At least not fought by humans."

"He's right," interjected my father gruffly, "there's no profit in it. It doesn't even work in principle."

"But if the reason was good enough – or the profit great enough –?"

"No, it takes too many resources, in too many places, and timed too well. Invade one reeking planet, and the enemy hides on another," Zachary explained. "Nuke it or gamm it and the planet isn't fit for habitation for centuries, anyway, so what's the carping purpose. Better just to negotiate a good deal and try to get along."

Claude finally grasped the situation. "Which is what The Old Man has been trying to do for years, but the Kozarians haven't been willing to talk until now."

"And he will do whatever it takes to keep the reeking Kozarians at the table."

"Which is why I need your help."

"Shad! Okay. Count us in," Dad said finally, speaking for the pair of them. "We'll need to get approval from our authorities."

"Already taken care of," I said. "I told you, I used The Old Man's clout. We're on the same timeline, now."

"I guess we should consider it a family trip," said my son.

I smiled through my doubts. "That's right. One big, happy family."

Chapter Five

Space folding is an arduous way to travel. Even without the disconcerting sensation of sight, equilibrium is thrown out of kilter when millions of points of light and gravity are spun together and one is thrown into the well between them.

You feel yourself ripped apart and slammed back together cell by cell and then the sensation begins all over again. And it goes on for hours.

Slowly, you begin to get used to it. Enough to squirm around and try to keep down some food, if you are able to find your appetite, too. After a day, some of the higher functions return, like the ability to talk without slurring your words or the ability to walk on two legs. Then, slowly, you begin to operate normally again, and eventually you may even decide that it is worth the several years you are saving on your timeline.

Maybe not.

I folded through space many times and found myself saying "maybe not" every time.

Yet, it saves time. And time has proven again and again to be the most valuable commodity in the universe. At least, I thought so. He who controls time, controls the galaxy, which is what The Old Man had been doing for centuries.

The first stage of our mission was to ferry the negotiating team to Kozar. We were assigned to a ship christened *"Cincinnatus"*. It was a little larger than a scout ship, with light weapons, a small passenger billet and fold drives. The party was given the option of stasis for the trip. All but one of the five chose the option. There were two women and three men on the team. The leader, Colin, chose not to take the chance that she would become a stasis casualty. I guess she figured that she was too important to lose and chose to tough it out.

She was as sick as the rest of us at first, but soon her attentions changed in manner.

"Excuse me!" She demanded once we had our instell legs beneath us. "Does the gravity have to be set so low? I can barely keep my feet on the ground!"

"Sorry, but this is the standard setting – "

"But surely, you can turn it up a little. I am used to standard Earth g's."

Zachary, who had spent more than half of his life in low g, turned on her quickly mocking her timbre. "Sure, we can turn it up until you're flat as a mackerel, but you'll find it a bit uncomfortable – "

I intercepted him before he could carryout his threat.

"I'll get you a gravbelt. You can simulate the gravity of whichever planet you like. The 'Earth' setting is right in the middle."

"Great." We turned to leave her but not soon enough. "Then if you could get me some tea," she added, "I'll be fine."

I wheeled back to face her. I narrowed my eyes but didn't speak what I was thinking. "How would you like it?" I asked.

"Piping hot. With a touch of cream, and a tiny splash of rum."

I was already sorry that I'd asked, but I tried to be accommodating. "We are fresh out of rum, I'm afraid...."

"Oh. Then a tiny splash of bourbon."

"Sorry – "

"Then Vodka? No? You must have some alcohol."

Zack was quick to jump in. "We have rubbing alcohol in the med kit. We can 'splash' that in for you." I shushed my father with a quick look.

Colin put on a sour face. "Just the cream, then."

"Anything else?" I asked, hoping that I wouldn't be sorry.

"A pastry or two would be nice. A croissant, perhaps."

"Would it?"

"Oh, it would be exceptional!"

"I'll check our stores."

Her attitude didn't sit well with us. We were used to far better treatment, and we had concerns of our own which went beyond trying to provide comfort for a person we considered to be self-important baggage.

We knew the importance of the mission and believed that in the end we would prove far more important than any of the negotiating party, but for the duration of the journey, we swallowed our pride and tried to make Colin comfortable. Thankfully, it was to be a short journey.

When we weren't serving the wishes of "her majesty", we were researching Kozar and its natives.

The colonies were just beginning to expand and

construction of The Hub was just underway when Kozar was discovered to be inhabited. The Kozarians were a spacefaring race of limited technology. They had been plying their way through the cosmos for a good many years when they ran afoul of the Shoorulians. For some reason, the two races just didn't get along. Having met the Shoorulians myself, I had a good feeling I knew why. Each stalled in their space exploration efforts – the Shoorulians learned a distrust of technology and became extremely isolationist; the Kozarians hated everything that touched Shoorulia. Humans would have steered clear of the conflict, except that their territories were right next to the heart of colonial space, and Humanity was already spreading well past the sensitive area.

The Old Man tried to negotiate with the Shoorulians and the Kozarians simultaneously. The Shoorulians reacted with suspicion, and the Kozarians reacted with anger. When they learned that we were talking with Shoorulia, the people of Kozar showed us the door and stepped up the war. At the time, Kozar seemed to have the upper hand, but that was before their sun began to act up.

It seemed that The Old Man had made the right choice in teaming with the birdfolk. That is until they acquired new weapons and used them indiscriminately against both Kozarians and Humans. When the Kozar sun went nova they took the opportunity to gain the advantage against their enemy. But their alliance with Humanity began to sour, too. The incident in which Stosh was killed was the last straw for both sides.

The incident also coincided with the acceptance by the Kozarians of a shipment of sight-restoring optics designed by Human White Coats. Designs based on the same technology with which I was able to see.

I had every reason to want the mission to Kozar to succeed. Success would break human connections with Shoorulia once and for all. *And to hell with them!* It would also give credence to the technology that enabled me to see, something which other Humans often found threatening. Also, it would give us a lead to find Trace, in whatever dire circumstance she may be in.

And it would put The Old Man in the debt column – a chip of unfathomable value in human space.

"There's not much about the Kozarians here," Claude was deep into research on the com terminal. "Apparently, there was little face to face talk when we first met them, and the files have not been updated recently."

"I downloaded all the information from The Hub," I offered.

"I've been through it. Still not much there. Most of the information is on the nova phenomenon. Techy stuff that goes back to almost the beginning of the fireworks. The phenomenon has proved to be extremely unpredictable. There will be a period of dormancy for days, or sometimes weeks, and suddenly the whole thing will flare up again – excuse the expression. Poor souls. Even a few seconds of exposure will cause permanent damage to their retinas."

"Any images?"

"Nova or Kozarian?"

"Save the flares for later. Let's see the aliens," I requested.

Zzkkkt-wwhhrr! I clicked on visual to inspect the pictures.

"There's just a few, along with biological information." Claude brought a still image up on the main view screen. "They're humanoid, almost mammalian. Males and females. Sexually compatible with humans, too."

"Hoozah!" exclaimed Zachary.

"The shower is down the corridor," I commented. "I guarantee its cold."

"Reeking sonic, too. Unfortunately."

"Strange information here, though," Claude went on.

"How so?"

"I've spent my life delving through information. The type of information someone decides to dig up can be as revealing as the information itself. This report about the biology of the Kozarians contains seven pages of general information – " Claude pointed suspiciously at the terminal. " – and five pages of specific information about their visual organs."

"They were studying the Kozarian's eyes? When was the information gathered?"

"Don't know. We would assume that it was provided after the sun went nova – otherwise why the detail on the eyes – so, it must've been furnished during a time when they weren't talking to Humanity. Considering the opportune timing of the eyepiece delivery, we have to make certain assumptions."

"The Old Man must have someone there, already."

"Or there's a Kozarian who is working with him."

"A plant or a mole?" I considered. "Interesting."

Claude was already thinking ahead. "The question is whether they will work with us, too."

"Or against us."

"They call the eyepieces 'Optics', although the White Coats prefer to call them 'Simulated Optical Neural Exchange Devices', or 'Soneds' for short."

"I think I'll call them 'Optics'. What else do we know about them?"

"Unique breathing apparatus. Their breathing is a separate function from any other. Means they can talk and eat and inhale and exhale at the same time."

I looked closely at the image on the view screen. I could see a couple of slits below the chin. "Are these them?"

"That's a couple of them. They circle the neck at intervals of about four inches."

"What about their hair?" It was actually more like a mane. It was the Kozarian's most striking feature. It was shocked and full of vibrant colors, framing the face like a halo.

"A unique feature, indeed. It is actually another sensory organ. And it apparently responds to stimuli. If you can learn to read it, you can tell if the subject is angry, sad, happy – "

"Lying or telling the truth?"

"Insufficient data."

Zachary peered closely at the alien image, trying to size up the life form. "Shad! Get to the important stuff," he said. "What's the quickest way to kill one of these things?"

"It doesn't say," Claude responded. "And that's not what were here for, anyway."

"But Dad's right," I said. "We need to be ready for anything."

Claude shook his head. He couldn't deny the possibility but was having trouble accepting it. He was still new to the game. "I can't say at this point. They are basically human. A boney skull protects their brains – If you can get through the cranium, it would be the quickest way to bring them down, but I don't know

67

how tough the bone is. They have a heart that is relatively protected in front, but more exposed in the rear. Best target, I guess, for a quick kill. Forget strangulation. You couldn't cut off all of their trachea, and their lung capacity is too great to affect a quick death. If they have an Achilles heal, it doesn't say in this report."

"Which doesn't mean they don't have one," reminded Zachary. "I can't wait to meet them."

I had to deny Zachary's suggestion. "Sorry, but that won't happen."

"What?"

"We didn't have time to implant your retinal shields. This ship's shields will protect your sight, but on the planet you'd be blinded. I need you here, anyway, to relay messages, run scans, and watch my back. You'll stay on this ship while I'm on the surface."

"You'll be alone. I don't like it," Claude objected.

"Yes. And I'll be stuck up here with your stuffy son! I don't like that either!"

"There's no other way. It'll have to do."

"Shad!"

The com line rang. It could be only one person. "Excuse me," Colin said.

"Your turn, Zachary –"

"Shad! This trip is not turning out to be very fun at all!" Dad stormed off to the harmless degradations inflicted by our lone, wakeful passenger.

Claude, at least, kept his mind on the situation. "When do you make planetfall?"

"Three days."

"Keep your eyes peeled."

"Yes," I agreed. "That's the plan."

Chapter Six

"They'll be here any minute."

We stood in the receiving area of the airlock. I allowed the beasties to rest. I was getting fond of life without the headaches that invariably followed prolonged prote activity. Besides, for the initial meeting, it was important to appear as one of the negotiating party – with all their limitations. The five of them would be blind until they were safe in the government building which was the only on the planet shielded from the excesses of the sun. There, the retinal shields could be clicked off safely, although the White Coats recommended keeping them in place for the duration of the stay just to be safe.

Colin demanded to be first in line, until I pointed out that she would be guiding the party through the narrow connecting tunnels and airlocks. Unless Colin wanted walk into a few walls on the way, it might be better to let me lead with proximity sensors in full sweep. She finally saw it my way.

The colonists were all successfully revived. They were still getting used to being out of cryo. I thought I noted a budding romance between a couple of the party, which might become complicated if their wives found out. I explained to all of them the effects of stasis obsession, and I thought again about Trace.

The things we do for love.

We finally got the signal that the Kozarian transport was approaching.

Zzzkkkktt-wwwhhhrrr!!

I threw myself backwards in surprise, colliding with the anxious Colin. I hadn't activated the beasties, but they were coming on-line of their own accord.

"What are you doing, Shicker! Get back up front. The Kozarians are docking!"

For a moment, the protes did their little dance. I could see light, but I wasn't prepared for it. It burst to life at once, not slowly the way I was used to.

I fell.

"Shicker, get up! Get up!"

"Watch it!"

I covered my eyes and rolled into a ball, shuddering with fear. What was going on?

Zzzkkkktt

I composed myself. Whatever was happening could be explained. I would just stand, get my bearings and pretend that everything was alright. My sight would be in use a few hours early, but that wouldn't cause a huge change of plans. Would it? I could run diagnostics later.

Steadying myself against the bulkhead, I wondered what the protes were up to. I got back to my feet and tried to compose myself, waiting to see.

Wwwhhhrrr!

Sight burst upon me. There was movement all around me. Figures I didn't know. It took me several seconds to realize that what I saw was not in front of my eyes. It didn't match what my proximity sensors told me. There were only two people in my vision when I knew there should be five in the room with me. And the people I saw were in front of me, not behind and to the side.

And they were not human.

I turned my head to try to right the situation, but changing my view didn't change what I saw.

Where am I? What the hell is going on?

"Shicker. What's wrong? You look ill." It was Colin's voice showing sudden concern, but the figure in front of me suddenly came briefly into focus. It was a woman. A Kozarian. But the beings from Kozar hadn't arrived yet.

The woman was saying something, but I couldn't hear her.

"Shicker! Open the airlock! They're here. What's the matter with you?"

I activated my other visual reactors, but that made things worse.

Zzzkktt- Zzzkktt-

It didn't make sense. Heat sensors showed the flaming bodies of the negotiating party around me. But it didn't jibe with visual scans, and the subcon trackers couldn't make sense of it. The figures left trailing, multicolored ghosts that the implanted computer tried to jibe with infrared readings, mistaking the surface lamp for one of the Kozarians. The result was a glowing face with exploding hair.

Zzzkktt- Zzzkktt- wwhhrr Zzzkktt- wwhhrr!

The image jumbled and fragmented and reassembled in nonsensical shapes and colors, directed by my implanted computer that continued to link conflicting bits of information.

Again, I stumbled and fell.

"My god, Shicker! Get up!"

"Kit. Are you alright?" It was Claude on the ship's intercom.

Then I realized that I was on the other side of the hatch. At least my vision was.

I concentrated on visual, turned off all other sensors, even proximity, blocked out the storm that was brewing around me.

The image was weak, somewhat blurred and jaggy, but it began to clear. The woman was gorgeous. Her high cheekbones and slight nostrils gave her classic human beauty. She could be human, except that her hair cycled through colors from bright blue to deep green and the tendrils seemed to have a life of their own, sometimes curling, sometimes standing almost on end. She wore an apparatus that covered her eyes, and her gown was low-cut revealing very mammalian cleavage. She and her companions were waiting patiently for the airlock to open. I concentrated hard on the vision. The details must be important – something I should remember, or maybe something I was dreaming. The woman turned toward me again. Yes, she was quite beautiful.

I was jarred suddenly. "Out of my way, Shicker! Where's that switch?"

I lurched toward the airlock and stumbled against someone. Disoriented still, I fell and collided with the bulkhead. Everything went black. Everything.

I passed out. Colin had to call for help from Zachary to open the airlock.

When I came to, I was on the landing transport enroute to Kozar. I kept all my sensors locked down, even proximity sensors and auditory reactors. I was afraid of being overloaded again but sight didn't return on its own. I sat silently.

"What was that all about, Shicker?"

"I don't know. A malfunction."

"Don't make me sorry we brought you along," Colin whispered. "You're supposed to be guiding us! They had to drag you onto their transport."

"I'll be alright."

"Well, you better shape up! We'll need you. We have to depend on you. None of us can see!"

"I'll be alright."

"Get ready! We're making planetfall, now."

Special Agent Shicker. Please log acknowledgement.

"Shicker?"

I must've gasped for a moment. It took me by surprise. This time, though, I knew the cause. It was a communication mode installed into my implants. I rarely used it. I preferred to speak commands instead of visually-typing them.

"I'm okay."

I closed my eyes to concentrate on the new task.

I M HERE. I M OK, I typed, selecting the characters one at a time from a menu superimposed on my eyelids.

Claude here. We discovered this function through the computer. We should B able to send/rcv messages between ship and planet. We didnt want to use audio in case sensitive parties might ?/overhear. What is your status? We R concerned.

I M OK, I typed again. It really was tedious. **I WILL MAKE AUDIO CONTACT ON THE SURFACE AND EXPLAIN.**

I began to think that perhaps the vision of the woman was a figment of my imagination. After all, the White Coats admitted that they had no idea how

73

imagination, dreams, and fantasies might affect the beasties or the control circuitry. It had never occurred before, but perhaps extensive pondering of the Kozarians had finally broken through some frayed wires. After all, the last image I saw before the breakdown was that of a Kozarian. I would get Claude to report to Walt at the earliest opportunity. Maybe he could make sense of it. But the speed of message transmission across instell was slow, and the reply wouldn't come for days.

I opened my eyes again. I was still blind though and saw nothing. Thank cod.

"We're here. Shicker, you'll have to guide us through the doors. Once inside, we'll be able to remove our retinal shields."

It was time. I scanned ahead with sonar.

The scan showed a large building made of a dense material a hundred meters or so from where we had landed. I suspected that it was shielded with titanium, although at this distance I couldn't make a solid read. The structure had no windows. The street before us was pockmarked with potholes and rocky debris – obstacles around which we would have to negotiate.

Inside the landing craft, the human party sat in a line behind me on the couch. They each had their left hand on the next member's shoulder. Someone must have instructed them that this was the best way to keep together. They were scared and helpless without their ability to see, all except for Colin who thrust a brave jaw forward.

The Kozarians must have been in a separate cabin. *Important trait to note,* I thought, *Kozarians are separatists at heart.*

"Prepare to disembark" came the accented voice of

a translator over the ship's com.

The door began to open. I grabbed Colin's left hand and put it on my shoulder. If this is the way they wanted it....

A Kozarian ducked through the doorway and presented herself.

"We're here. Just a few steps and will be in the building. Stay close. We'll assist as we can. Watch your heads."

Another Kozarian made sure each party member ducked through the low door. I followed the woman closely and moved slowly allowing the train of humans to find their footing and carefully skirted the obstacles that my scanner had spotted. The air smelled like vinegar. We were the only ones on the street.

The lead Kozarian turned to me, but I kept my head down, scouting the safest route to the door of the government building. She started to speak and then thought better of it and turned back to her course to the door.

We finally arrived, and another Kozarian helped each of the humans over the threshold. As the party entered, I activated visual.

Zzzkktt- wwhhrr

Nothing unusual happened. The pixels bloomed in the manner in which I was familiar. I was relieved. I briefly noted the streaked, nightmarish sky that cast green hues on the surfaces of the buildings. There were occasional flashes of orange. I was the first human ever to see the spectacle, thanks to the beasties.

I waited for the last of the party to enter before stepping across the threshold. The door was sealed behind me. Tightly. Against the sun, I supposed, but I felt like a prisoner.

Dim, yellow artificial light illuminated the room. The beasties adjusted quickly.

"We're safe now," commented the Kozarian woman. I stared at her silently.

Colin spoke out to her mates. "Don't drop your shields yet. Wait 'til we're further inside."

We formed our mule train again. The Kozarian turned to me and spoke.

"I hope you have recovered. There was such frightful confusion trying to get you all through the airlock."

"I'm very sorry. I'm so embarrassed."

"Don't be. We hope the rest of your stay won't be quite as – strenuous."

I found myself staring at her again. "I'm sure all will go well from here."

She smiled at me gently. "I'm sure."

She took my arm and led me through another door into a long corridor. The rest of the humans followed dutifully and without incident.

"I'm D'Awlia. I'll be your party's liaison."

"I'm Kit. Nice to meet you. Thank you for your understanding hospitality."

I felt a sudden tug from Colin. She, apparently, wanted to make the formal introductions. I ignored her. I had other things pressing my mind.

D'Awlia was the Kozarian I'd seen in the airlock. In my vision.

It wasn't my imagination after all.

Chapter Seven

"Tell Walt, we've got a problem," I whispered over my private communicator to my son. I was sure that the line was secure – and I had done a comprehensive scan of the location – but I felt I needed to be extra safe.

I was in my private, windowless room. It was comfortable but sparse. The bed was soft though, and the shower used real water.

"I must have picked up some kind of interference from the Kozarian eyepieces. I actually saw what one of their group was seeing. It fooled with my sensors and caused an overload. It zonked me good."

"We'll let him know. It'll be awhile before we get an answer –"

"I know, but send it soon. We're in trouble if it happens again."

"That girl seemed quite concerned. Very attentive to you. I'd get close to her if I were you." It was Zachary butting in, reading implications into the situation.

"Forget it. I've got enough to worry about."

"The best way to get information – "

"I said forget it. Get that message to Walt. And tell The Old Man the party is here. The first meeting is tomorrow."

"Will do," said Claude. "Anything else?"

"In an emergency, the beastie link – I mean the visual data link – is the best way to get in touch. I doubt that anyone could tap that line."

"I'm glad we uncovered it. We asked the computer for options to get a message to you, and it revealed that data line."

"I'd forgotten about it myself."

"You are full of surprises, aren't you?"

"I continually surprise myself. Keeps life interesting, I suppose."

I signed off and looked over the schedule for the next day. Satisfied that I had nothing important to do, I left the room. I went to Colin's quarters and invited myself in. She was still rubbing her eyes.

"Everything is so bright," she complained.

"Your pupils need time to adjust. Try some more eye drops if it keeps bothering you."

I turned on full scan and searched the room. It was clean. No bugs or other transmitting devices that I could spot. I couldn't penetrate the walls with sonar or any other sensor, but if I couldn't, it was unlikely that anything the Kozarians had could either.

Colin understood what I was doing and followed me from corner to corner.

"I told the others not to say or do anything until you checked their room."

I just nodded. The room was clean. I left and checked the rooms occupied by the other humans. Nothing.

I had just searched the last room when I spotted D'Awlia at the end of the corridor. She came toward me, and I stopped to let her catch me.

"Kit. Everything check out?" She knew I had been to see the other humans and probably guessed my real function. One of them, anyway.

"Yes. Everything seems fine. The accommodations are excellent."

"Very good. Is there anything else?"

"Yes, as a matter of fact. I'd like to see the meeting room, if I could."

"Certainly. This way.

She led me to an elevator. It was large enough to carry all of our team and more. I kept my deepsight in place for the route, but found no surprises.

The elevator opened, and I was led down a short hall to a double door. There was a guard posted outside.

"The conference room is underground, so it has extra protection from the nova. There are no windows of course, and this is the only way in or out."

"May we go in?"

"Yes, but first you must surrender your weapons, temporarily."

I nodded and removed the laz from between my fingers.

"I forget that it's there," I admitted honestly as I handed the weapon to the Kozarian guard. D'Awlia just smiled.

The room was like any human conference room. It had a large table in the middle and room for a gallery on one side. The gallery was vacant of chairs for now. If progress was made, I imagined that they could fit in a hundred or so onlookers, if necessary. The room scanned clean. It had even been scrubbed with an ammonia-based cleaner, which I smelled even before I sensed the chemical traces.

"Looks good," I said. "I'll go over it again tomorrow, of course."

"Of course."

We left the conference area, and I reacquired my laz.

"If you have time, Mr. Shicker, I'd like to show you something else."

"I guess I have time."

"Quickly then, we'll have to hurry." She began to sprint like a schoolgirl toward the elevator. I had to hurry to catch up with her before the door clanged shut.

We ascended several floors to an observation platform on the roof. There were various antennas affixed on rotating platforms, all pointed towards their sun that was rapidly setting. We were alone.

"I know the sun won't kill your sight, mine is already dead, so I thought it would be safe to bring you up here."

"I'm here." I did a quick scan of the rooftop, walking around the edge. The antennas were transmitting EM, but otherwise there was nothing of import. The streets below us were lifeless.

She came up behind me. "But look over there." D'Awlia pointed toward the horizon. "Watch."

I looked where she pointed. The sky that was streaked blue and gray before began to transform. I turned off all modes except visual and saw an amazing spectacle.

The sun lashed out like a light-saturated paintbrush and dazzled the atmosphere with a myriad of colors. I saw the tongues of the nova lash out violently, but what it touched was metamorphed into a beautiful array of light. Soon the sky was a mosaic of blues, pinks, and yellows, blending into one another in a splendorous work of color. It went on for several minutes as the sky began to darken.

Then sunlight began to fade. The nova still struck out from the heart of the sun, but now it left only darkness. Soon the sun and its rays disappeared from view. I realized that D'Awlia's arms were around me and her head was on my shoulder. I didn't complain, but in the back of my mind, I had the idea that I should be faithful to Trace.

But Trace was not part of the present. She was a memory that called to me from my past, and a ghost that I would pursue in my future. I didn't even know if she was still alive.

No, I knew that she was alive. Somehow I knew, but there was much I needed to do before I would see her again.

"Beautiful, wasn't it?"

I admitted that it was.

"Imagine that I grew up, never knowing that the sun could do that. Create so much beauty," she whispered. "Your Human inventions gave us that. That sight.

"Before I could see, the sun was an enemy. We huddled in caves, afraid of the daylight. An entire planet blind. Only our outer colonies saved us from the Shoorulians. They waited at the edge of our system waiting for the sun to stop flaring so that they could swoop in and eliminate us. We would be helpless to defend ourselves without sight.

"Your optics brought us new hope."

I stood silently. I wondered if she understood the price. Everything has a price. The Old Man would be sure to exact his.

He was still collecting from me.

"I will do everything I can to make this treaty happen." She looked at me with determination. "I don't want to lose this gift you brought us."

"Sight?"

"No. Hope."

I removed her optics. She had large, almond eyes that were beautiful by human standards. I stopped thinking and turned off visual scan. I kissed her.

It was the best way to get information, I justified to myself.

Chapter Eight

The arguments raged by day. The nights were filled with passion. D'Awlia and I kept our affair quiet; although she assured me that it wouldn't matter to her superiors. Neither of us were decision-makers in the negotiating process, and Kozarians had an open policy regarding relations between consenting adults of any species.

"We are only asking for free passage through your system and a couple of outposts to regulate trade," Colin would proffer.

"Humans are uncontrollable. They multiply like 'rabbits'!" (I substituted an Earth equivalent for "Wh'Lokeru" to understand the metaphor) "It is impossible to stop their spreading once they get a foothold in system. We'd be lucky if they didn't take over Kozar eventually." These were the main arguments used by E'Lowa, one of the leaders of a Kozarian faction.

"But Humans can supply us with these sight-giving optics! Without them, our people suffer. Will continue to suffer! With them, our people will be productive again, and we'll have a chance against the Shoorulians." This being the response by his Kozarian opponent,

K'Mack. "They are not asking that much in return."

"Any concession is too much. Our sun could stop flaring at any moment. We wouldn't need the optics. We would need nothing from Humans." This from the head of Kozarian government, P'Clellan. "Of course, the sun might keep acting up. Regained sight would make so much easier. Our people will live fruitful lives again. The economy would blossom."

Inevitably P'Clellan would say, "Perhaps we should talk it through some more."

It was comforting to see that Kozar government was much like Earth's used to be. Of course, Humans no longer inhabited Earth, and The Old Man had all but eliminated all opinions but his own from Human Interest. But it was no small wonder that Humans had sacrificed their self-rule in favor of a seemingly benevolent ruler.

I stood in the gallery and watched the discussion move back and forth and tried to stay alert. Every once in awhile, D'Awlia would flit in with some important papers or a message or just to provide a diversion for me. Or so I imagined.

After hours, the trysts were adventures for D'Awlia and me, exploring alien anatomies and making amazing discoveries. She could sustain a kiss indefinitely, thanks to her unique breathing apparatus. I learned that her hair was actually a form of villus, highly sensitive tactile organs. Stroking her hair would bring her to a frenzy of desire.

After a few days, I could add volumes to the brief Kozarian physiology described in the library information.

When he learned of my relationship with D'Awlia, Zachary hooted and hollered like a lunatic. I tried to

84

explain that it was only to gather information, and he laughed all the more. Claude was a little more circumspect. "I don't like it," he told me.

"Oh?"

"I think you should be concentrating on your mission. The sooner it is accomplished, the sooner we can find Mom."

"I'm not even sure what my mission is," I scoffed. "The Old Man only told me to keep my eyes open."

"Exactly."

"Are you sure that you just don't want your father 'fooling around' with another woman?" I asked. "More than ten years has gone by on my timeline since I last saw Trace."

"I just don't like it, that's all."

Claude's comment ended our discussion.

On the third day of talks, I received a message.

Kit. Pls respond via audio com. Claude.

I left the talks and went to my quarters. I scanned the room quickly in case there were new bugs. Once again, there were none.

"Kit here."

"Walt responded to your previous message. He says that he sees no reason why the soneds – or optics, whatever – would be interfering with your implants. He'll do some tests and get back to you. However, he says to avoid prolonged exposure to the inadvertent vision. It will (quote) 'blow your mind' (unquote). Something about how the brain can't process conflicting bits of information. Neither can your interface," I was hoping for a little more detail, but this was all my son could relay at this point. "Oh, and if it happens again, he wants you to report back. If you can."

"Hopefully, it won't happen again."

"How are the negotiations going?" Claude asked.

"Hard to say if there's been any progress. It seems like Human Interest is losing out, though."

"The Old Man won't like that."

"I suppose not, but it seems that the Kozarians are getting used to their blindness. Enough so that they don't want any incursions from human colonists."

"Kit," it was Dad breaking into the conversation. "How the piking much longer will we be here?"

"Hard to say. They are some who are still trying to convince the leadership that it's worth reconsidering."

"So there is still hope?"

"Yes."

"And we're sticking around?" They were getting antsy.

"For awhile longer."

"Shad!"

I returned to the proceedings and noted that nothing had changed since I left. I felt obliged to leave sensors operating and keep my eyes open. I was contracting severe headaches. The beasties were getting their revenge for being put through their paces for extended periods of time. I decided I would shut them down as soon as the meeting adjourned and wouldn't bring them up again until the following day. The evening's anatomy lesson would be conducted in the dark.

"Do you think we're related," D'Awlia asked.

"Um, er, I hope not, but I'm learning my family is full of surprises."

"No, I mean Kozarians and Humans. We are so much alike."

"Not if you ask E'Lowa."

"Male and female. Biologically, anatomically,

we're almost identical. Do you suppose the same amino acids which started Kozarian life could have formed humans, too?"

"I don't know if that's how it works."

"Perhaps it was a biological seeding program. Some ancient alien race created the genetic code in amino acids it launched on comets throughout the galaxy – "

"You're full of crazy ideas, aren't you?"

" – Making us alike in so many ways."

"The most important ways."

"In some of the little ways, too."

I was learning crucial facts from D'Awlia, too. Little things at first, but I was making progress, and I was barely trying.

I learned that Kozarians and Shoorulians once shared the same planet. The Kozarians left and made Kozar their home world. Shoorulians coveted the new world and the conflict began – or probably continued. I assumed they didn't get along in the first place or the Kozarians never would have left in the first place.

The government building in which the negotiations took place was once a prison. I suspected as much. The rest of the city was deserted.

D'Awlia told me about the flares. "The records from the early days are hazy. It was very unexpected. We knew as much about our sun as any race. We studied it and sent probes as close to it as we could get. Nothing predicted that anything unusual was about to happen. Then, it started. It was long before you or I were born."

"That may not be the case with me. I'll have to check my timeline. I think I was born about when the flares started."

"Then maybe you are a jinx. Bad things happened as a result. Millions of people died, not directly as a result of exposure to the sun, but because they were blinded. We were a highly mechanized society. Suddenly, no one could see. Many people died immediately in accidents, others as the society and economy broke down. Hundreds of thousands died of starvation. More of disease. We were thrown into a primitive state. It was years before we began to recover. Now, our children are raised in caves away from the sun in order to preserve their sight for as long as possible. Few make it to adulthood without exposure to the flares, though, and they are destined to live in darkness anyway. It is a horrible existence, but now you've given us hope. We'll be able to see again."

"What if the flares stop?"

"It's true, we haven't been able to mount much of an effort to put an end to it, but it may not be ideal if they do stop. We know the Shoorulians are waiting to march in as soon as the flares subside. If we are blind, then we can't defend ourselves. It's as simple as that. The optics give us a little help there, but I don't know if it's enough."

Virtually all of the Kozarians lived underground to avoid the sun, but most were blinded eventually. Only a few moments of exposure burned out their retinas that caused the blindness, and few could avoid the sun forever. They cultivated a mushroom like fungus that was the new staple in their diet. Most green food grew well under the nova, but few Kozarians were willing to work the fields to bring the crops in.

The first Humans to visit Kozar took advantage of their hospitality and their promiscuity. That was years before the sun went nova. The Humans were ejected as soon as it was learned that we were treating with Shoorulians. There was no further contact between the species until a Human ship landed with the sight granting soneds. It was an offer that couldn't be ignored, but while Humans still had relations with Shoorulia, no aid was accepted. That changed just days later. Humans were invited to the table, but the establishment was resistant to grant Humans any concessions at all.

In return for her information, I was trying not to say anything of value. It was difficult to discern if she was even trying to get information from me. She certainly wasn't pressing for it and didn't seem to care whether I talked about Humanity or not. I gave her a brief history of Earth and the beneficence of Humankind. I was careful not to mention Humanity's imperialistic tendencies. I never mentioned The Old Man.

The beasties had been coexisting happily with the Kozarian optics, and I began to think that the first incident in the airlock was a fluke. But that evening, it happened again. This time I was more prepared.

Zzzkkkt-wwhhrr!

It was another grainy image. I saw K'Mack and one of his assistants, K'Croft, sitting at a table. It must have been a civil discussion with whoever was originating the broadcast. K'Mack was smiling and leaning back; his hair relaxed. He exchanged remarks with K'Croft.

Instead of reacting quickly, I took my time. I decided that in order to trace the problem, I needed to find the source of the transmission.

"Where is K'Mack?" I asked D'Awlia.

"I don't know. Why?"

89

"I need to find him."

I was already at the door. My blind training taught me to count the steps from the bed and memorize the position of the furniture. I turned on the proximity sensors to their lowest setting.

"I wouldn't go out there wearing that."

"Wearing what?"

"Nothing."

"Quick, get me some clothes."

She bunched a ship suit into my arms. I had picked up the laz on the way to the door. I didn't imagine that I would need it, but prudence suggested that I take it along.

I groped down the corridor, soft sonar giving only a foggy indication of the walls of the corridor. D'Awlia dressed and came up behind me.

"Let me help you. Where do you want to go?"

"I don't know. I have to find K'Mack."

"We left him in the conference area. But that was hours ago."

"Wait a minute." I stood still and concentrated on the image I saw. "I see a green vase or sculpture...." It was hard to tell. The image was extremely low resolution and the transmitter moved just when I got a fix on an object. "It could be sub-meeting room or someone's quarters."

"There are a hundred rooms like that in this building."

"I know. Wait. There's a basin in the background. It's somebody's room."

"That reduces the number by about a dozen. Eighty-eight rooms to go...."

"There's a colorful picture on the wall – a portrait! No, that's somebody else there, in the background.

Wait! Damn! It's gone."

The transmission phased into the visual spectrum of the hallway in front of me. I turned to D'Awlia.

"Quick! Go find K'Mack! Tell him this is urgent!" It was urgent. If this kept happening, it would interfere with my mission. I would be too easily distracted. I might miss important details – of whatever it was I was supposed to see. I needed to find the source of the transmissions.

"I can't do that!"

"Of course you can! You're the delegate's liaison."

"Not his delegation!"

"This is important, damn it!"

She left for the nearest com port. Not knowing where else to go, I followed, hoping that the image would return.

D'Awlia spent a few moments in desperate hushed conference. Eventually she turned from the com and told me that K'Mack was in a confidential conference. His whereabouts was a secret. It was a momentary dead-end, but I knew I would have the answer soon enough.

The next day I was surprised to find a message waiting for me from K'Mack. Our contact to this point had been limited to gripping and grinning in greetings and salutations. It was as much contact as I had with any of the Kozarians, D'Awlia excepted. He summoned me to meet him in his quarters before the morning conference.

I was there promptly; full scans (and laz) in place.

K'Croft opened the door and bid me enter. I did a preliminary deepscan of the room, trying not to be obvious. All seemed in order. I looked around for a green vase, but I found none.

"Mr. Shicker! I'm glad you had time to meet with me. Please sit down."

I took a seat at a small round table. Wrong size and shape to fit the vision I saw the night before. That pretty much answered one question I had. This was not the room I had seen in the vision.

I thanked him and refused a drink that K'Croft offered.

"I heard that you were looking for me about an urgent matter," K'Mack began. "I had been meaning to talk with you, so I thought I should take the opportunity to converse with you. Perhaps our two purposes are really the same." He brushed his mane back from his face. His hair lay limp behind him. I had learned that this was a sign of frankness among the Kozarians.

"Perhaps." I decided to let him lead the conversation. I didn't have anything to say. Yet.

"You've been in the conference all this time. I don't know if you are following the procedures, but it is beginning to look as if P'Clellan is going to reject the Human proposal."

I shook my head. "That is too bad." I noticed that K'Croft was standing at the back of the room. I shifted my chair so that I could keep track of him better. I also had the subcon trackers mark him as a priority target in event that things were to become violent. Best to be prepared.

"Many Kozarians would be displeased with this development. I believe there would be open rebellion. Your devices mean that much to our populace."

"How many have been given to your people?"

"No one has them but the people in this building, and they will all be returned if Humans are asked to leave."

"That may not be necessary."

"It is how Kozarians do things. We have no choice. It is our way."

I understood. The Kozarians pride themselves on their independence and their self-determination. Earth was like that once.

"Perhaps you could come up with a device of your own."

"I'm afraid it is beyond us. We don't have a background in the science of amoebic electronics, and without sight, I doubt we could make the necessary advances."

"I'm sorry, but I don't know how I can help."

K'Mack stood and walked around the table. He went to where K'Croft stood and poured himself a glassful of blue liquid. He held the decanter up to the light, studying it closely. "That simple task – pouring a drink, is much easier than I ever imagined it would be – with eyes that actually see. I know that you know what I'm talking about. Let's forget about all the beauty that we never see – mountain vistas, the moon over our blue sea, the smiling faces of our children. Appreciation of beauty aside, we are incapable of performing all but the most simple tasks because we simply lack sight." He turned back to me. I waited for him to make his point. "Mr. Shicker, you are a very special person. We know about your abilities. We know that you've spent most of your life without sight. And we know that you were relatively happy. Then you had the chance to see. You were like we are now."

"Yes?" I didn't know where he was leading. What did he want of me?

"We are getting desperate. I've used every

argument I could think of. P'Clellan is weighing our arguments fairly, but I'm convinced that is the opposition that needs to come around to our way of thinking. I want you to try to convince E'Lowa. If he consents, then we will have a consensus, and P'Clellan will have to rule in our favor – for Kozar's best interest. In the Human Interest."

At last. I had been waiting to discover the real reason the Old Man wanted me on Kozar. This must be it. But how long had he been working to set this up? It was such a simple, reasonable request. Is this all there was to my mission? There must be more to it than that.

"Remind him of the beauty in the world. Remind him of the productive, satisfying lives –"

"Your people seem to be leading productive lives now. They don't consider themselves handicapped. They have adapted remarkably, admirably well."

"But given the choice, you chose to have sight. This is a choice that they should have, too."

I felt that I should push back from the table and pace the room to consider the request. It was a simple request. One that I'd be willing to do on my own. For Humanity's sake. For Kozar's sake. But it felt like a trap.

I leaned back in my chair and pushed the hair back from my face.

"I'll do it," I said.

K'Mack set up the meeting for that evening after the latest round of talks. At the conference I watched both Kozarians carefully. K'Mack was getting desperate. He practically pleaded with P'Clellan to give the humans a chance. Colin even chimed in that human outposts could be manned mostly by Kozarians, with checkpoints and safeguards to be regulated by Kozar. Trade incentives would also be granted.

"You don't understand!" E'Lowa exclaimed. "We don't want ANY humans in our space!"

I would be an interesting meeting with him tonight, I thought.

Kit, pick up com. Urgent.
B RIGHT THERE.

It was shortly after the mid-day break. I excused myself and noted that K'Mack and E'Lowa watched me closely as I left the room.

"Kit, we received an urgent message from Tom," Dad was manning the com.

"Tom? Who's Tom?"

"How the carp would we know?! It's your message!"

Zachary was getting cabin fever. His limited patience had worn through.

"Read me the message, Dad."

"It reads: 'To Special Agent Shicker, Warning. Unauthorized human renegade locked to your heading. Extremely dangerous. Avoid contact *AT ALL COST*. Tom.' 'At all cost' is emphasized."

"That's a message I've heard before."

"This time, you can do something about it."

"Keep a wide sweep of the area. Let me know if a ship unfolds nearby."

"Of course."

"I'd feel a little better about this message if I knew who 'Tom' was."

"Kit, it's Claude. I just reviewed this urgent message. You should know that the message was signed with the initials 'T.O.M.', not the name 'Tom'."

"Shad! Same difference, my insolent Grandson!"

"It is not the same difference!"

"Learn some respect for your progenitors!"

"Cut it out, you two. We're almost through here! I think we've reached a breaking point in the negotiations. One way or another, I think we'll be done here soon."

"Thank cod! I can't stand to be cooped up here with this reeking, old – "

I cut off the com early. I'd heard enough to know that my back-up was nearing the breaking point. I could hardly blame them. I was sick of the negotiations myself. Maybe I could make a difference tonight. Maybe E'Lowa would listen to me.

In the meantime, I had another thing to worry about. A human ship locked onto my last heading, apparently meaning personal harm to myself. Why? There were probably a dozen humans who would wish me ill, but none that I knew of who would venture into forbidden space for the chance to get at me. Maybe this was a carry-over from the Shoorulian incident and the loss of "the item". I knew only that it could complicate the Kozarian mission.

And who the hell was "T.O.M"?

Then it came to me. "T.O.M." stood for "The Old Man"!

This was a serious complication, indeed.

My conversation with E'Lowa did not go well.

"I've heard all the arguments before, from people I respect more than you."

"You don't know me," I said.

"You're human, I know that. Therefore, you are not to be trusted."

"That is a snap judgment."

96

"But it is fair. Actions speak clearly, Mr. Shicker." His mane actually bristled, the hairs standing out from their sockets like daggers. "Look at your species' past. You ruin your home world and then move on. You ruin those worlds and then move on. The story is the same everywhere you go. You spread like a virus until nothing else can live with you. You conquer through association and leave destruction in your path."

"I'd like to think that we have bettered ourselves."

"Humans have yet to prove that they have."

"We hope to make a start by offering your people something they need."

"You haven't heard what I've been saying. Association with Humans pollutes. Any association! I feel dirty just talking to you!"

That was getting too personal. Unnecessarily so. In other circumstances I'd have dropped the furhead. I felt my toe unconscious treading near the laz's kick safety. I composed myself and reentered the fray. If this was my purpose, as an unofficial negotiator, I needed to make the most of it.

"What assurances do you want? What can we offer for the sake of Humanity to show our good faith and foster goodwill between our peoples?"

God, I sound like an automaton. I am out of my league. Why isn't Colin here?

"There is nothing you could say because your word is meaningless," he snarled. "I would rather die than see my people mixed up with your kind. Taking anything from Humans is the same as death!"

"You've lived in the darkness too long, E'Lowa. You don't know what dying is."

I turned to leave, and found the door already open for me. At the last moment I searched for the green vase I had seen in the short vision the day before. No, this wasn't the same place.

"Shicker!" I turned when he called my name. There was something flying through the air in my direction. My arm rose reflexively, and I aimed the laz between E'Lowa's eyes. I stopped myself at the last instant before I depressed the trigger. The Kozarians were surprised to see me pointing at him. Proximity sensors kicked in, and I caught the optics E'Lowa had tossed in my direction.

E'Lowa recovered enough to say, "Take these things back. They've clouded my vision long enough."

I stepped through the door, and it closed behind me. D'Awlia was waiting for me there.

"Any softening of his position?" she inquired.

"No. In fact, he has been restraining himself in conference."

She sighed. Behind her optics, I could tell she closed her eyes, as if reminding herself of the darkness which was waiting to take hold of her species again. "There is still hope. You've got to talk to P'Clellan."

"I'm sorry, but I think I'm just making things worse."

"No. He is reasonable man. He wants to do what's right and will listen to all sides. Talk to him. I know he will listen to you. He must."

Old Man, you picked the wrong person for this mission. I was a man of action. Words just didn't accomplish anything for me. I needed to use my fists and my weapons to fight for what is right. Words and logic weren't sharp enough. I couldn't wield them with enough impact. They didn't cause enough pain. I would do what was right, but on a battlefield not around a conference table. I would rather be carried from the war as a casualty than walk from a treaty in shame. I knew the price there was to pay when life was at stake, but I couldn't wage this kind of war.

But I had to try. I owed Humanity that. Kozarians deserved my best effort, too.

"I'll talk to P'Clellan. Set up the meeting."

P'Clellan's room was larger than the others. His office was connected to the corridor by an antechamber in which I waited. His room was flanked on either side by K'Mack's and E'Lowa's. The set-up reflected Kozar's parliamentary government. Each faction was granted equal status, but one leader made the decisions.

I waited impatiently for my appointment. We were approaching a critical point. P'Clellan had finally announced that he was close to a decision. Colin was sure that we were on the wrong side and insisted that she accompany me to see the Kozarian leader. I was both relieved and insulted by the suggestion. True, Colin had more experience in these things, but it could be restrictive in subject matter and tone.

Fifteen minutes after the meeting was scheduled, P'Clellan finally called us into his office.

Colin began to speak first, but she was silenced immediately by a wave of the Kozarian's hand.

"Excuse me, Colin, but I've been hearing you speak for the past week. Mr. Shicker has yet to say a word. He called this meeting. Let's hear what he has to say."

I wasn't prepared for that, but I did my best.

"You've heard a lot about Humanity the last few days. I suppose it is all true, the good and the bad. But I think there are really just two issues to keep in mind. We need a route through this sector of space. We don't need more colonies in this area. Not really."

I could feel Colin's glare fixed on me. A Human colony in Kozar space was a point she had been pressing for since the beginning. Any progress she might have made may have just been undone. But I continued, hoping that I wasn't causing irreparable harm.

"The bigger issue is: what do your people need? They are surviving now, but they have been robbed of one of their senses. We can help to give it back. Not because we want something, but because Humanity at heart is a compassionate, sympathetic species. We want to help. And if in helping we are fostering understanding and better relations with Kozar, then we are a step closer to what we need."

"Mr. P'Clellan, I want to say that Mr. Shicker is a generous person, but he doesn't necessarily speak for Human Interest – "

Again, P'Clellan raised his hand. "I understand, but please let him continue. Go on, Mr. Shicker."

"E'Lowa says that your people don't need sight. That has been proven to be true, and I can understand. I was born blind, and I was raised to believe that it didn't make a difference. I could function almost as well as a sighted person. Better than some, in fact. But then I was granted sight. I had to be taught every color, every shape, every nuance of sight. And suddenly, the Universe expanded in ways I never thought possible. Every new thing I see makes it grow a little larger still.

"I don't know how well our two peoples will get along. Maybe we don't treat outsiders too well, but we haven't been treated well ourselves at times. Let us at least make a compassionate, no-obligation, gesture to help yours and maybe we will all take a step closer to greater understanding. It's worth a try, isn't it?"

100

"You make some good points –," P'Clellan seemed touched by my suggestion and threw his mane back in a grand gesture of acceptance. " – But it seems to me that if we take these optics, we become obliged to and maybe a little dependent on Humans. How long could we depend on your 'goodwill'?"

P'Clellan leaned back to hear my answer, and I started to say "Forever", but Colin interrupted me. I was thankful that she did, because the situation began to get complicated.

Zzzkkkttt-wwwhhhrr!

Colin explained that the treaty terms would insure a long, continual relationship with checks and balances and would be mutually beneficial and so on. I saw her at the edge of my sight, but suddenly that vision was overridden with a grainy, head-on glimpse of her speaking. I froze.

The angle of the new vision coincided with P'Clellan's position. I was seeing through his eyes.

I allowed the image to consume my mind. I hoped for some insight into the leader, but in the end it was just an image. At one point, he turned to me. I saw myself concentrating with my eyes closed. He/I didn't let his gaze linger on me, so I assumed that he accepted my posture. I/he looked back at Colin as she finished her remarks. I noted in the background a green vase and a washbasin. This was the place.

A few seconds more and the vision faded. My eyes were my own again.

P'Clellan agreed to give what we said his full consideration. I wondered if we had made any progress, but Colin seemed happy. I remained silent as we left his rooms.

One mystery answered, but was this an advantage? Or a curse?

Chapter Nine

"We've got to be able to turn this to our advantage." Claude was always thinking.

"I'd like to know how."

"Spy on the opposition?"

"To see what?"

"Um, clandestine plans to overthrow the empire?"

"Maybe we could get information that we could bribe P'Clellan with. Force him to accept the reeking Human treaty." Zachary was thinking along a different line.

"I can't imagine how that would work. I doubt if I'd see anything worth extorting him with in the next couple of days. I don't even know what Kozarians find so reprehensible that he'd want to cover up. And I'm sure that trying to manipulate him that way would backfire in the end."

"What is he doing now? What does he see?"

"I don't know. I can't just turn it on and off."

"How is it happening? What's causing it?"

"I don't know. I wish I did."

"This is not a piking great advantage to us."

"Frankly, I'd be happy if it never happened again. At least I'm handling it better, now," I admitted.

"Anything from Walt?"

"No," Claude responded. "Nothing more from The Old Man, either."

"So, we are back where we were."

I closed the com link. We had one more day of conference. It was a formality. P'Clellan had asked the principals for private meetings, and afterward, he would make his decision which would be announced the next morning.

Colin thanked me for my participation, but I couldn't tell if she really meant it. I didn't know if I'd made a difference. I hoped so. At least they would be winding things up. I was anxious to leave and see if The Old Man had any information for us regarding Trace. D'Awlia and I had already discussed my departure. We would miss each other, but there were no hard feelings. We understood that our destinies lay light years apart.

And with any luck, I would be out of the system before the pursuing renegade could catch up to me. Until recently, I could trust my luck, but I couldn't shake this feeling of dread.

D'Awlia and I spent a pleasant evening together. We talked a little about our separate lives. I never mentioned Trace, but I think she knew that I felt a commitment elsewhere. She was destined to remain on Kozar, and she was committed to help her people whether or not the optics were left behind.

At some point we stopped talking and shared her bed. There was nothing more to say.

The next day's conference was filled with empty pronouncements of friendship, progress made, and new understandings between our people regardless of the decision that P'Clellan made. It made me think back to my own words with P'Clellan. *How foolish I must've sounded,* I thought. I was surer than ever that Humanity had lost this bloodless battle.

I was trying to come up with a strategy to convince The Old Man that he should still help us find Trace when my data receiver blinked on.

Kit, Urgent. We need you here at once. Dispatching personal transporter. Get back here!

I hastily left the conference area and retrieved my laz from the guard. When I boarded the elevator, I tried to open the com line, but there was no response. I turned the protes to full scan mode, but I didn't need the beasties to tell me that there was trouble on the ship.

As I was leaving the building, I noted D'Awlia in the doorway. She must have noticed my expression as I left the conference. I waved for her to return inside as I called the personal transport to my location. I looked back as I stepped into the man-sized vehicle, but she was gone.

The transport closed as soon as I entered. I ordered it to launch directly and take me back to my ship, but instead of moving vertically it followed a parabolic path and zoomed low over the landscape.

"Computer, where are we going?"

"Destination is set as the town of Barkhoh on the planet Kozar. Coordinates –"

"No we aren't! Take me back to the ship –"

"Destination set and cannot be altered without authorization."

"Computer, implement emergency override codes: Alpha, Bravo, Gamma – "

"Improper overrides codes."

Damn it!

I tried to alter the vector manually, but I was locked out. I examined my surroundings.

A personal transport was basically a human-sized crate. There was only room for one inside. It was one of the most common conveyances in Human space. There were millions of them, but they were all basically the same. The sides were cushioned, and the controls were free floating so that they could be repositioned comfortably. There were internal grav controls that could be altered to simulate a standing or reclining environment. There was a tiny view port, but it wasn't commonly used. A vid scanner could bring a view to the screen on the control panel. Other simple scans could also be performed. It was designed to carry a person a short distance, even out of a planet's atmosphere, comfortably, albeit unglamorously.

This transport was practically new. It was not one of mine. I had been shanghaied.

I remembered The Old Man's message. *So much for avoiding contact at all cost,* I thought.

I tried to radio for help, but I was not allowed access to the com. Even the beasties' data link was being jammed somehow.

Someone had intercepted my call for a transport and sent one of their own. He must've been waiting nearby. I hoped I would get the chance to meet the bastard face to face. I tried to send another message, although it wasn't directed to anyone in particular. I figured that who ever had kidnapped me was listening.

The com blared to life. "Special Agent Shicker. You have vital information for me."

"Who is this?"

"Not important."

"What do you want?"

"Not now."

"When?"

"Soon."

Soon, we hovered momentarily over an abandoned village. The town was in ruins, but a small tower presided over the town. It was one of the few structures that still stood above ground. The transport veered to the top of the tower and landed. The door opened. I did a final scan and stepped onto the parapet, vowing never to reenter the vehicle.

Circling the building on the rampart, I found nothing unusual. There was a dusty doorway on the opposite side. I went inside.

The tower was a narrow cylinder and stairs that negotiated a tight turn down through the interior. An orange glow from the setting sun infiltrated the windows and a number of holes in the wall. The structure appeared empty. I still had full deepscans operating and kicked off the safety of the laz. The air was thick with ash, and I could smell the residue of a recent fire. I quickly found the source of the stifling air. The steps had been blown away to the first landing. Someone wanted to keep me at the top of the tower, but who ever it was, they didn't know Orphans or their standard planetfall equipment.

I stepped back outside. Maybe now, I could find out what the bastard wanted.

A voice spoke from nowhere.

"I'll bet you're wondering why I asked you here."

"I'll bet you're wondering how I knew you were going to ask that?" I said.

I spotted the transducer. It was a grape-sized remote, ordinarily used for exploring dangerous, hostile environments. Operated from a low orbit, it was virtually indestructible. It could be armed with low powered weapons too, so I assumed that it was dangerous. I had the subcon tracker target the device, but there was little hope of causing it any harm.

"You have information that I need," it said in its squeaky, mechanical voice.

"Let's start with the important stuff. Who are you?"

"I'm asking the questions! I want to know what you know."

"I'm a pretty smart guy. I know a lot of things. You'll have to be a little more specific."

"I am missing a very valuable commodity. You know where it is."

I moved a little farther from the grape. I was at the edge of the wall. I looked over the edge at the ground a few hundred meters below me. "I still don't know what you're talking about."

"Well, that will be cleared up when I know what you know." I began to hate that phrase. There was a noise from the tower.

"My transport is your only way out." It loomed like a standing coffin where it had let me disembark. "You have no choice. We'll have a quick conversation then I'll let you go safe and sound. Once I find what I'm looking for."

"Couldn't we just have a friendly little conversation back at my place?"

"I'm sorry, but I wouldn't believe anything you'd say without taking certain measures."

Certain measures? I didn't like the sound of that, either. "I'm a very trustworthy person –"

"No."

From the tower door a couple of meters away, a device hovered into view. It looked like a stainless steel helmet designed for a human head but the inside was covered with needle sharp probes. I had heard of such contrivances that were designed to extract thoughts and memories directly from a person's brain.

"A crown of thorns. For me? You shouldn't have."

"Put it on. You have little to worry about. People seldom emerge with brain damage. It is even rarer that people die."

"Thanks for the opportunity, but I think I'll pass."

"Get in the mindcap. Now!"

To emphasize the command, the grape blasted a portion of the wall to my right. The wall disappeared in a blaze of argent light. My shield might take one shot like that and hold. Maybe one.

"Kill me and you will never find 'the item'." I took a chance. It was hard to believe that the incident on Shoorulia was still pursuing me, but I couldn't imagine what else could be implicating me. "I don't think it even exists anymore. 'The item' was destroyed."

"That's what you want people to think. I've learned different."

"Sorry, but you are mistaken." I noticed that the grape had slowed down slightly with the manipulation of the mindcap. My adversary must be controlling both at the same time. A loner. It opened up some options for me.

"Get in, or I'll blast you over the side!"

I moved to the gap in the wall and put my hands out to my sides in a gesture of surrender. "Then shoot, if you dare. I'm not putting that thing on."

There was no response. I shrugged and shook my

head. "I thought so," I said and then pointed at the grape as naturally as I could. "You don't have the guts." I squeezed off a shot that hit the grape dead center. I was proud of the shot, but didn't take the time to admire it. I was too busy falling off the side of the tower.

My left hand moved to the dial on my belt even before I jumped. As I fell, I quickly switched it to its lowest setting and floated the rest of the way down to the ground. Subcon told me that the grape had been stunned momentarily. When I disappeared from its sight it searched the perimeter of the parapet and then moved back into the tower. It then plummeted over the wall searching for me.

The grape had been designed for systematic surveys and methodical searches. Although it was fast, its abilities fell far short of competent in the hunt and pursuit category. It didn't have the ability to maneuver after a quick-moving object. I had only to keep moving and wait for help to arrive.

Help? I'd almost forgot.

DAD! I NEED TRANSPORT. CALL DAWLIA & TELL HER 2 BRING A KOZARIAN TRANSPORT 2 THIS POSITION. DONT SEND 1 OF THE SHIPS. ON 2ND THOUGHT, TELL HER 2 THROW 1 IN THE BACK.

Where R U?

I DONT KNOW. TOWN CALLED BARKHOH. TRACK MY LOCATION BY ORIGINATION POINT OF THIS MESSAGE. SEND HER 2 ME. TELL HER 2 BE CAREFUL!

I quickly circled around the tower as the grape looped the perimeter opposite of me. It had almost caught me when it suddenly gave up and zoomed off toward the nearby, low-slung buildings. I moved off in the opposite direction and found a comfortable looking cave to hide out in. It looked as if it had been inhabited recently. There were shards of glass brushed into a corner, and the dust was impressed with a number of footprints.

Dawlia is on her way.

TELL HER 2 LOOK 4 A CAVE OPPOSITE THE TALLEST TOWER IN TOWN. TELL HER 2 B READY 2 LEAVE AT ONCE.

I noted the grape's location on subcon. It was getting closer, and it was learning. It was making a grid pattern search. The area it was searching was getting dangerously close to my location. There was only one exit, and I would soon be forced to leave, or I risked being discovered. I watched from the doorway as the grape turned away for another sweep which would bring it closer to my location.

Dawlia is nearing your location. Approach instructions?

TELL HER 2 LAUNCH TRANSPORT & LAND NEXT 2 TOWER ON MY SIGNAL.

I waited for the grape to move to the farthest point of the sweep from my location, then I ran for the tower. The remote must have sensed the movement because it turned and tried to track me in quick pursuit.

NOW!

It was gaining fast. My original intention was to swing around the tower, almost in a full circle to lose the device which I knew to had difficulty maneuvering, but speed itself was the deciding factor and that point was in the grape's favor. I changed plans instantly and ducked into the interior of the tower. My new tactic gained me a few valuable seconds.

I leapt up the stairs, taking as many as I could at a time. I quickly found myself at the first landing above which the stairs were still smoldering from the remote's earlier blast. But I didn't hesitate. I leapt into midair, dialing the gravbelt as low as I could. A moment later, I crashed into debris on the other side of the tower, but I hadn't reached the top of the steps. My shield protected me from the worst of the impact, but the smoldering wood of a side beam burnt my hands. The narrow, winding interior made it difficult to maneuver to the next landing above me. Subcon told me that the grape was then gliding carefully after me. I had to hurry.

With my belt still rendering me practically weightless, I pushed off and up through the tower. I flew through the air, my neck colliding with the top landing. Again, my shield protected me, but I had to make a quick turn to catch hold before I fell. I silently thanked the inventors of the gravbelt. I was clinging by the very tips of my fingers – an impossible grip to hold if I'd been any heavier.

I hauled myself up and noted the grape's position. It moved slowly and carefully up the winding steps, bouncing between the walls when it moved too quickly. I waited until it was at the first landing, almost directly below me. Then I stepped back and lazzed the remaining landing, standing supports, and any debris I could find. My purpose was not to destroy anything, merely to fill in as much of the inner tower as I could. Sonar in affiliation with other elements of my deepsight had already picked out the major stress points, so it didn't take long to accomplish what I had set out to do.

Once I was sure that I had buried the grape deep in refuse, I jumped off the tower again. D'Awlia landed within a few meters of me with the door open and beckoned to me. I ran quickly to her and heard an explosion behind me. The remote was trying to blast its way out, but was merely causing more of the tower to fall on top of it. By the time we launched, the grape had managed to slug its way out, but it had a difficult time getting its new bearings. Before it could find us, I ordered my personal transport in the direction of the remote, hoping that the grape would follow it instead of us. It worked. The Kozarian transport zoomed off for the horizon, leaving Barkhoh far behind and the grape even further afield. I was free of that little problem.

At least for the moment.

D'Awlia was worried about leaving at a critical time in the negotiations. I assured her that I would have her back to the capital as soon as I could.

"What was that all about anyway?"

"I'm not sure. Somebody has it in for me, though. They think I know something."

"What do you know?"

"Nothing."

"Doesn't seem like anything they should get excited about."

"That's what I thought."

On the return we flew low over the landscape in the Kozarian transport. The land was lush. It would have been a productive area if it could have been worked effectively. Soon we passed over an area that was divided into thin rows by intersecting cords. It surprised me to see that there were crops ripening in the field, and D'Awlia pointed out a solitary figure tilling the soil. It was the first Kozarian I'd seen outside of the government building. Further on, there were several more working down the aisles of green slowly, methodically, one hand within reach of the cord on either side. I detected a series of tones coming from the blind Kozarians. An identification device or sonar emitter, I supposed.

"See what we are reduced to? Pathetic isn't it?" D'Awlia commented.

I thought it was rather admirable.

On the way back to the capital, I received a call from Claude and Zachary over the ship's com.

"What did the reeker want, anyway?" Claude asked.

"Some information. I'm not sure about what. Maybe 'the item' that Stosh blew up on Shoorulia."

"That won't do him much good."

"He doesn't seem to know that."

"Get back here soon. We want to clear out of this reeking system."

In the back of my mind, I wanted to get my hands on the intruder, but I had to admit that it would be better to be done here and get back to our search for Trace. "Yes," I agreed. "I'll second that."

Colin left a message in my quarters that I read as soon as I arrived back in the governmental building. She and the other humans were having a get-together in her room. A celebration of sorts. She invited me to have a few alcoholic drinks with them – an old Earth custom. I thanked D'Awlia for watching my back and went to Colin's quarters. I desperately wanted to give the beasties a rest but kept deepsight up in spite of a developing migraine. I heard the celebration inside when I reached her door.

"Come in, Kit. I can call you Kit, right? The party's over, so the party is just beginning, so we don't need to be so formal anymore, okay? So, start calling me 'Colin', okay?"

"I've been calling you 'Colin'."

"Well then I'm way behind you, aren't I?" She was

pitching dangerously back and forth, and I held out an arm to steady her

"You're way ahead of me as far as the drinking goes."

"So I am," she laughed, "but that will change!" She stumbled to a makeshift bar where two of the other humans were mixing drinks. One of them offered me a "frosty grunge like they make it on Parma." It was pink and cold and potent, so I sipped it slowly.

"I guess you're all ready to leave, huh?" I asked.

"Yes, it's been a tough couple of weeks, but we've made progress. I can't wait to report to The Old Man."

"Oh? I wasn't sure that we had changed P'Clellan's mind."

"Me either. I thought we were close, though. But K'Mack came to see me after his meeting with P'Clellan and told me that there had been a breakthrough. He said that the decision was made to grant humans limited access to Kozarian space. We're in, my boy! P'Clellan is breaking the news to E'Lowa now."

"Boy," commented one of the human bartenders, "what I wouldn't give to be there now!"

Zzzzkkktt-wwhhrrrr!

Suddenly, I was. As if on cue, my visual scan phased out to be replaced by an image of E'Lowa. I quickly shut down my other sensors and stumbled back toward the door.

"Whoa lookout!"

"What was in that grunge?" There was laughter. It was a strange soundtrack to accompany the image I saw.

E'Lowa was madly shouting at P'Clellan – but it seemed like he was shouting at me. He looked strangely naked without his optics, but his blue,

115

sightless eyes screamed violently. His mane was writhing wildly like angry snakes. Hands – P'Clellan's hands – reached out to steady the Kozarian, but E'Lowa pushed them away.

"Take me to P'Clellan's. Right now! I need to go."

"Steady, my boy. He's in a meeting."

"I've got to go. Where's D'Awlia?"

P'Clellan needed help. I had seen E'Lowa get angry, but this was something different. He was mad beyond reason. Enough to kill to keep humans out of Kozarian space. I sensed that something awful was about to happen.

I tripped over something and fell, my head hitting a table on the way down. I pulled myself back to my feet and groped for the door.

"Cut him off!" somebody chuckled.

"He looks hurt. Maybe we should get someone – ."

I rubbed my head. A nasty lump was growing where it had smashed against the table, and there was a little blood, but none of that would distract me. "No! Just take me to P'Clellan!"

"Alright. Somebody take his other arm."

I was half dragged into the corridor. Once there, I could stand easier. I allowed myself to be led in the direction of the elevator. It was progress, but I wanted to move faster.

"Let's go. Hurry!"

I saw something menacing. It was just a glimpse, but I was sure that I'd seen it. Something sharp and lethal. E'Lowa was trying to hold it out of sight, but I knew it was there. I hoped that P'Clellan would see it in time. The leader's hands reached out again, to calm him, but E'Lowa struck with the dagger. The razor-edged point seemed to strike right in my face.

I screamed.

"Hurry. He's being attacked!"

"Who? Who's being attacked?"

"P'Clellan!"

"You're crazy!"

I broke away from them and beamed in proximity sensors. I was able to concentrate on sonic enough to get to the elevator, ignoring the vision as best as I could.

On visual, I was aware of flailing strokes trying to find me. One or more found their mark. There was blood on the floor and splattered around the furniture. I saw elderly hands try to grapple with E'Lowa, but he was younger and stronger.

"No!" I exclaimed as the elevator finally opened. "Get away from him! He's blind! He won't find you! Help is on the way!" I tried to remember the way to P'Clellan's. Left. No, right!

"This way," Colin directed impatiently. She took my hand and guided me down the corridor. We still had a distance to go, and there was little time.

A dagger lifted in to the air. My eyes followed it faithfully, mesmerized. I couldn't turn away. Couldn't blink. Couldn't flinch. Then it descended. In slow motion, the way things happen when time is meaningless, when fate has turned a card, and there is no stopping the inevitable. The dagger struck my chest. Deeply. And it was left there as the room wheeled about me. As my sight dimmed, I saw E'Lowa run to the door, past the green vase I saw so long ago in another vision.

I screamed. I don't know for how long. I was still standing, my vision slowly phased back to normal, and proximity sensors showed me a clear path ahead. I jumped down the hall, past Colin, running as fast as I could. I turned a corner, and found P'Clellan's antechamber door already open. There was a guard inside and another coming from the corridor in the opposite direction. I pushed my way in. The office door was still closed, and the guard was preparing to kick it in when the door began to swing inward.

The guard grabbed the Kozarian standing there. He made no move to resist. In his right hand, he limply held a bloody dagger. I was ready to strike E'Lowa, the man I had just seen raise a knife and plunge it into my chest. But the Kozarian coming from P'Clellan's chamber wasn't E'Lowa.

It was K'Mack.

Chapter Ten

A trial was scheduled. The Kozarians strongly urged (to the point of demanding) that everyone in the building at the time of the murder be present at the trial. The legal procedure on Kozar required that parties connected to a crime be present at the corresponding trials. At times this must have meant that whole communities were embroiled in issues of law. In this case, only a hundred or so would be involved. It was phrased as an option for us, but because the outcome was so crucial to Human Interest, the negotiating party would have decided to stay regardless.

K'Mack was charged with murder. He was found in the dead man's room with the murder weapon. He had the opportunity.

"They say that he wanted to force the Kozarians to treat with humans." The motive.

"We have witnesses that say that P'Clellan had already agreed to allow humans a foothold in the system."

"Those are people that K'Mack told. E'Lowa hotly disputes the claim."

"He would, of course."

"E'Lowa says that P'Clellan had told him that he

was going to send the humans and the optics back to The Hub," said D'Awlia.

"P'Clellan only talked to the two of them that night. First K'Mack, then E'Lowa."

"So it is just the two of them and their words."

"And an eyewitness." Me.

"You've got to testify."

"I want to, but there are witnesses who know that I was in another part of the building when the attack occurred. How can I say that I saw what happened?"

"Did you see it?"

"Yes!"

"Do you have any doubt that E'Lowa murdered P'Clellan?"

"No!"

"Then how can you sit by a let K'Mack be convicted? Don't you know what's at stake? If K'Mack is convicted then rule of the council will be turned over to E'Lowa. You know what that means. No Human contact. No sight for my people!"

"It means more than that."

"What more is there than that?"

"You don't understand. I saw E'Lowa kill me. Kill ME!!! I saw the knife sink into my heart. I felt the blade twist in my chest. I felt life drain from my body. I bled! It was as if he was killing me! Me! I want justice. I don't give a damn about the treaty. I'd kill the man with my own two hands if I had the chance."

"Then we've got to get you on the stand. We've got to convince the judge that what you saw really happened."

"We need P'Clellan's optics."

"What?"

"If we could show that the optics were acting as a

120

transmitter to my vision receptors then we should be able to convince the judge to allow my testimony."

"I'll see what I can do," D'Awlia called on her way out of the room. "Wait here."

I wasn't going anywhere.

P'Clellan's soneds were evidence, so the authorities were unwilling to let it out of their hands. They would allow certain experiments to be conducted by their examiners, however. We just had to determine what experiments they would be. Until the trial began however, the optics were to be left untouched. We queried a test for the earliest opportunity. It would be performed soon enough.

"Who is being charged in this court of the people?" One of P'Clellan's chief assistants, D'Rab, was licensed as a judge and had seniority in this vicinity. He would reside over the trial.

"K'Mack of the lineage K'Lach," answered one of the guards.

"What charges are being brought against K'Mack?"

"He is charged for the murder of P'Clellan."

It was a formal open to an informal trial. Kozarian law allowed everyone a voice, and the people followed very strict rules of order and evidence that kept the proceedings from becoming fiascos.

"What is the basis for the charge against K'Mack?"

One of the guards who discovered K'Mack at the scene was the first to speak. Traditionally, it was the police's function to announce the cause of the arrest. "Your honor, I found K'Mack at the scene of the crime. He was leaving P'Clellan's office with the murder weapon in his hand."

"As presiding judge in this arena, I, D'Rab, declare

that preceding's against K'Mack will commence at the first light of our next day and will continue on succeeding days until I am satisfied with the quality and quantity of evidence. All parties who have evidence to present will prepare themselves to offer it on behalf or against K'Mack or both as rules allow."

I had no misgivings. Although I wasn't present in the room in which P'Clellan met his demise, I felt personally involved. I could almost feel every blow that was struck. In my mind, I could still see the final, killing blow. It was as if I had been murdered, not P'Clellan. And it galled me that E'Lowa, the man I had seen use the knife against me had not been charged with the crime. If he had, I might have been able to hold back and not give testimony. But now I felt I had a duty to perform. For justice.

Later that day, I came across E'Lowa. I could barely contain myself. Under different circumstances, he'd be begging me for his life, but in this instance he had the audacity to approach me with an air of confidence. I saw again in my mind's eye the image of E'Lowa, with his blue eyes blazing, raising the knife and plunging it into my chest. I formed a fist and waited for his approach. A member of E'Lowa's party hung close by his side in case he needed assistance.

"Mr. Shicker, I've heard that you believe that I'm responsible for P'Clellan's death. That doesn't surprise me."

I looked down at him. He was quite a bit shorter than I was. I expected to be met by the same glaring eyes I had seen in the visual scan, but E'Lowa was wearing his optics once again.

"It doesn't surprise me that you would lie for your

cause," he said.

"We'll see who is lying," I replied.

"The surprising thing is that you didn't kill P'Clellan yourself. That would be a more human way of accomplishing your goal, wouldn't it? Why are you relying on K'Mack to do your dirty work? Wouldn't it be more efficient if you alone killed our leader and then lied about it? Fewer people involved?"

"Everyone here is involved. Everyone on this planet is involved. If P'Clellan hadn't been killed, then Human and Kozarian interests would now be tied together. You stood against that, so you murdered him. When the evidence is heard, you'll be sorry that this trial is taking place."

"I AM sorry that this trial is taking place. The sooner humans leave our space the better."

"In the meantime, I see you've allowed yourself to use one of the human devices which you so despise."

"The technology I like. It is the source of it that I despise. I'd rather not be wearing them at all, but it couldn't be helped. There is some evidence that I need to go over for the trial. I need my sight to examine it. Have no fear, though, as soon as K'Mack is convicted, I'll be ridding myself of these things forever."

"I'm sure that you will."

"By the way, have Colin pack early. As the new leader of Kozar, I will expel your party as soon as the trial concludes."

"We'll see if you're still leader then."

We turned our backs to each other and marched off in different directions.

A few hours later I went with D'Awlia to the guard post that was holding the evidence for the trial. They allowed us to view the evidence in a cubicle at the rear

123

of the post. A technician, W'Lillad, hovered over us as we went over the knife, the autopsy report, and the contents of the room, including P'Clellan's personal items. We weren't allowed to touch anything. W'Lillad held the items which we wanted to examine and manipulated them as we instructed. We turned to the soneds.

"We've got to see how these are different from the other optics. I never received any vision from anyone else on Kozar. If we can determine how it is different, then we may be able to reproduce the condition that broadcast the sights I saw. We would be able to make a strong case for allowing my testimony."

The first thing we noticed was the soned's size. P'Clellan was one of the largest Kozarians in the building. He was even taller than me, so its huskiness was not surprising. It also looked a little cruder than the one that D'Awlia wore. The reservoir holding the protes was blockier and jutted out from the ears in a conspicuous manner.

"That's right," D'Awlia remembered. "He was one of the first to receive the optics. Right off the delivery ship, in fact. The human who brought them wanted to make a quick impression on him."

"So this must be one of the first prototypes. Let's take a closer look."

I asked the technician to hold the optical device closer to me and to turn it slowly. I made note of several characteristics under full scan and then asked D'Awlia to do the same with her optics.

I looked between the two a number of times before I spotted anything of significance. Under x-ray, I noted a hairline crease along the side of the prototype. It could have been a crack, I thought at first, but it extended too deep in the forged alloy body. D'Awlia's optics were solid at the same point. I marked the point on subcon and examined the opposite side. There was a matching crease on the opposite side of the prototype. I marked the second crease with a subcon tracker and compared the placement of the two creases. It was too uniform to have been caused by accident. Looking deeper, I noticed that the crease led to a terminal circuit. I had no idea what any of the circuitry did, so it may not have been significant, but it gave us a place to begin.

"There are two abnormalities here and here. It may be nothing. Could you put the optics on for us?"

W'Lillad complied. He switched his soneds with the pair last worn by the Kozarian leader. Again, I compared the two with full scans operating. I could see nothing unusual between the two.

"What could have triggered the vision?"

D'Awlia just shrugged.

"The first vision I saw happened as you were arriving at my ship. He may have been excited then. The next time, there was a conversation with K'Mack. It seemed cordial enough. Then the last time was when he was killed. What is the connection?"

"I don't see any."

"Then it must be a random event. We may never reproduce it."

"Then K'Mack will be convicted and E'Lowa takes control of the council. We can't have that," she said as she brushed her hair back with determination.

"No, we can't."

The next day at the trial more evidence was mounted against K'Mack. E'Lowa presented first.

"P'Clellan first met with K'Mack, then he met with

me. He told me that he was going to expel the Humans and end the treaty negotiations. He must have told K'Mack that he had made the decision. Shortly after my meeting with P'Clellan, K'Mack returned and killed him."

There were objections from several points in the gallery.

D'Rab acknowledged the objections. "Unless it is confirmed by further testimony, court will consider E'Lowa's testimony regarding K'Mack's actions as speculative." The gallery quietly accepted this judgment and the trial continued. There was no further evidence to authenticate E'Lowa's conjecture, but there was plenty of circumstantial proof corroborating what he'd said.

The fingerprints on the knife (admittedly, not as indisputable as with humans), angle of the attack wounds, and blood on K'Mack's clothing all pointed to one Kozarian as the killer. The court was adjourned for the day with a strong case damning K'Mack.

I slept fitfully that night and had a vivid dream of the murder. It seemed so real. Once again, I saw E'Lowa's eyes burning with rage. The vicious knife attack trying to find its victim. The final plunging blow. I awoke in a sweat.

There was no chance that I would fall back asleep, so I dressed and wandered about the building. I found myself back at the guard post. I requested to see W'Lillad. I waited a few minutes before he appeared.

He was groggy, but patiently agreed to demonstrate the evidence again. I glanced through the evidence again. The blood stained knife, the shards of green glass found on K'Mack's clothing, the soneds. I stared at them a long time, hoping that they would reveal their hidden secrets.

I knew what I'd seen, but the truth remained hidden.

W'Lillad donned the optics again. I found the creases in the optics but couldn't see their significance. He operated them again, but nothing happened. I had him push, pull, slide, tweak, and turn the device, especially in the area of the creases, but nothing happened.

I was suddenly aware of a new presence in the room. It was a bleary-eyed K'Croft who was on a similar mission as my own.

"There seems to be a preponderance of evidence against our man."

"I can't believe it's true. I've worked for K'Mack for more than twenty years. I know he is dedicated to his cause, but he would never do this."

"When I testify –"

"No one will believe you. Not unless you can prove that you can see through those optics. Strength of your belief alone won't sway the judge."

"I know. I am beginning to believe that I did dream it all. That maybe I wanted to see E'Lowa kill P'Clellan."

K'Croft blanched when I said that. "You must not say that! You must not even think that! We need you. K'Mack needs you. There must be justice!"

I just shook my head. "I'll do what I can."

"K'Mack will get a chance to tell his side tomorrow. If there is no new evidence by the end of the day, then the trial is finished. K'Mack is finished." There was a long pause. He wearily turned and trudged out of the room.

"Kozar is finished," he sighed as the door closed.

We had just one day to find the key to P'Clellan's optics.

Chapter Eleven

"I spoke to P'Clellan, it's true," K'Mack revealed. "I was sure that he had decided against us, but instead he told me that he was going to grant my party's request to give Human's access to Kozarian space and more importantly, he was going to allow our people to accept the optics. Kozar would see again!"

"Lies," uttered E'Lowa.

"Silence!" warned the judge. "Let him speak in his own defense."

"I could barely contain myself," K'Mack continued. "I should've stayed silent, I know, but I couldn't help myself. I went to tell Colin right away. I told K'Croft, too. I asked them to quietly spread the word. I was thrilled, but apparently E'Lowa wasn't as happy about the ncws."

E'Lowa remained silent, but he shook his head. The entire room knew what he was thinking.

"I returned to my rooms and began to write a synopsis of the main points to be covered by the treaty. Then I heard a noise. There was a crash – like something breaking. Then a startled scream. It sounded like it came from next door. I ran to P'Clellan's door. I fell against someone fleeing the scene. I didn't get a good look at him, but a moment later, I heard E'Lowa's door close."

"Do we really have to listen to this garbage?" E'Lowa asked.

"Go on," D'Rab directed.

"P'Clellan's outer door was ajar, so I entered. It was dark, but there was light coming from the office. I went inside, and there was P'Clellan lying on the floor with a knife in his chest. I don't know. I thought maybe he wasn't dead, that I could still help. I pulled out the knife, but it was hopeless. Next thing I knew, there was a banging on the door. Eventually, I opened it, and I was charged with this awful crime. I wish that P'Clellan had not been killed, but most of all I wish that Kozar would be receiving the optics as he wished and which now certain parties," a look in E'Lowa's direction clearly indicated to whom he was referring, "are refusing to grant."

The judge called for evidence confirming or repudiating his claims. There were plenty of witnesses to confirm that K'Mack had indeed told several people that Kozar would be accepting the Human proposal. Others had heard the crash and the scream, but none saw K'Mack or E'Lowa enter or leave P'Clellan's rooms.

The court adjourned for a late lunch. My turn was next, but I was afraid that I would convince no one. I wasn't sure I had the heart to do it.

D'Awlia and I went back to her room. We sat silently for a few minutes.

"You'll do fine," she said, trying to encourage me with forced enthusiasm.

"I'm not afraid of my performance. I just know that no one will believe that I saw what I saw."

"If you say it with enough conviction –"

"No. It's not enough. We need to demonstrate that what I saw isn't just in my head."

She pushed her hair back in the calming gesture that I had begun to notice among the Kozarian. I had a brief thought, but it fluttered away before I could grasp its meaning.

"Let's go back. I'm doing no good here."

Outside the courtroom, refreshments were being served to everyone involved in the trial. We passed on the offered food and returned to our seats. I had to think through what I was about to say. I barely noticed when the proceedings began again, but when the judge asked for more testimony in the defendant's behalf, I stood almost automatically.

"Your honor, K'Mack could not have killed P'Clellan. I saw the whole thing. I saw who killed P'Clellan and it wasn't him. It was E'Lowa!"

The crowd in the room was in a furor in a second, but I didn't wait to hear the objections. I forged ahead.

"I saw the entire thing through P'Clellan's eyes. I don't know how it happened. I don't know why it happened, but I saw it all. E'Lowa was in P'Clellan's rooms. E'Lowa was yelling at P'Clellan. He was incensed. Crazy. His hair was moving, like it had a life of its own." The gallery seemed to understand what that meant. They murmured and nodded to one another. "Then he pulled a knife. He began to strike with it."

"D'Rab this is ridiculous. This human shouldn't even be here! This is none of his affair! We don't need to listen to his lies!" E'Lowa said.

The judge silenced him with a gesture. I continued.

"P'Clellan tried to block the attacks, but E'Lowa kept coming. Then, I saw him raise the knife – " I looked up as if there was a knife suspended before my eyes. I held my hands up to the spot then dramatically lowered them to my chest. " – and he plunged it into my chest. I mean, P'Clellan's chest. Then he fell to the floor and E'Lowa ran from the room."

The room was silent. I let the drama hold for a second then continued. "As I've said, I can't explain how I saw it. It might have been some kind of malfunction from P'Clellan's optics, I don't know. But I know what I saw. It was E'Lowa who was there that night, not K'Mack. I swear it. You have the wrong man on trial."

With that, I sat down. Some in the gallery seemed to be swayed, I wasn't sure that D'Rab was.

Someone began to laugh, and then clap his hands. It was E'Lowa. He stood and asked permission from the judge to refute my testimony. When it was granted he walked over to my seat.

"Congratulations, Mr. Shicker, that was quite a performance. Tell me, do you act outside the court room, or only when Human Interest is at stake?"

"I saw what I saw."

"Humans have a vested interest in this region of space, don't they? K'Mack has a vested interest in seeing the Humans stay here. Ask yourselves what would happen if P'Clellan had announced that he was barring Humans from Kozar. Who would have lost out? Why would I kill the leader? He already told me that he was siding with my arguments."

He turned to the judge to deliver the rest of his speech. "Now, we have a human who not only says that K'Mack is innocent, but he tries to implicate me in the murder. He knows that I am the most influential opponent that he has here. In one swift moment, he negates the decision and neutralizes his opposition. He is trying to turn the advantage to the side of Humanity. Are you willing to do that? Let him railroad this result after the decision had already been made to expel the humans? Think before you side with him. Think about what he is trying to do. Think about what he has to gain."

"I saw what I saw," I said.

"It's a lie."

"I saw – "

"You saw what? You saw me kill the man? Show us again what you saw. Stand up and show us that final, dramatic knife plunge."

D'Rab nodded to me, and I took the floor, raising my arms above my head –

But E'Lowa grabbed my elbows. "You saw me strike downwards? Like this?" He put his hands over mine. He could barely reach them. Together, our hands struck toward my chest in a downward motion.

"How could I have done this? P'Clellan was a few centimeters taller than you. Was I standing on my tiptoes on the top of a chair?"

"Maybe he was on his knees."

"You don't know? You claim to be there and see this dramatic event, but you don't know what position he was in?"

"From my view – "

"Oh yes, from your view. You were looking through P'Clellan's eyes, right. Okay, look through my eyes. I'm wearing optics now, look through them and tell the court what you see."

"I can't."

"Go ahead, I give you my permission."

"I can't turn it on like that."

"You can't? Isn't it convenient that it happened to turn on just as he was about to be killed? Isn't it convenient that you happened to see your opponent committing a capital crime? Might I suggest that you saw exactly what you wanted to see! D'Rab, please disallow his testimony. It is a lie and an insult to our system of justice."

D'Rab considered for a moment. "I am predisposed to agree with E'Lowa. Witnesses, even eyewitnesses are inclined to put a subjective slant in their interpretation of facts. Yet, I see in your conviction a belief in what you saw. Can you prove that you have this special sight?"

"Your honor, I'm trying now to recreate the circumstances –"

"If you can prove that you are able to see in the manner you described, then I will allow your testimony. Otherwise, it will be disregarded. I will give you until tomorrow morning to provide a demonstration."

That was that. The court was adjourned. I succeeded in putting off the inevitable for one more day. It was small consolation.

D'Awlia tried to sooth me, but I pushed her away, telling her that I was sorry, but I needed some space to think. And some time. Always more time.

She sat on the edge of her bed and pushed her mane back and then curled her locks forward before pushing them back again.

I was learning that mane manipulation was as much a part of a Kozarian's mannerisms as any human hand gesture. The reflection hit a chord somewhere in the back of my head – a thought that had slowly wormed its way to the surface.

"Wait. Do that again."

"What?"

"That thing with you hair?"

She blushed. Manes were a very private item in the Kozarian physique. "This? Just this?"

Her hair fell partially over her soneds. A little further back, and it would be in line with – *That's it!*

I grabbed her arm. "Come on. Quickly!" I dragged her through the doorway and sprinted down the hallway.

"Where are we going?"

"We're going to do another test on those optics. See if I can get the sight back."

I released her and allowed her to keep pace with me as best as she could. We were back at the guard post in a few minutes. W'Lillad was there faithfully manning his post. I asked him to brush back his mane. He gave me a similar reaction as D'Awlia had. "This is important. Let it fall just behind the ears. No, no. Push it toward the creases. I've shown you where they are."

He made a clumsy gesture to follow my instructions, but it didn't work. I turned to D'Awlia. "Help me think! This is a nervous gesture that I've seen many Kozarians make. They try to force themselves to relax by pushing their hair back like this." I demonstrated with my own hair. "But it doesn't go far enough. The villus, the hair, has to make contact with these points here." I pointed to the handles on an imaginary set of soneds. "What mannerisms do Kozarians have which would do that?"

"Regaining composure – after an argument?"

135

offered W'Lillad.

"Try it," I requested. There was a subtle difference with the earlier mannerism. Nothing.

"Anything else?" I looked from one to the other. "Think! P'Clellan was a leader. THE leader. He was in charge! I received the visions before he met me in the airlock, when he was meeting with K'Mack, and just before he was killed. What gesture might he perform in those situations?"

She didn't move a muscle as she thought hard. "W'Lillad," D'Awlia directed. "Pretend that you are important. You are nervous, but you don't want anyone to know. You want to show your are in command, but you want to seem relaxed and ready for anything!"

He performed the gesture. If there was a difference, I couldn't tell, but D'Awlia seemed satisfied.

"Very good! You should be an actor! Now, pretend that you are challenged. A new species is about to be encountered, an underling has suggested that you aren't looking out for your people, someone has threatened your life! Now, do it again!"

W'Lillad straightened his back slightly and in a short, sharp stroke, brushed his mane behind his ears.

Zzzkkkttt-wwhhhrrr!

The beasties contorted themselves and my point of view rotated 180 degrees. In a grainy image, I saw myself wince slightly.

We've done it! Now, let them try to refute me!

I got on the com to Claude. The demonstration was planned, but I felt a sudden need for more information.

"We've got to find out if this is intentional or not? Is this an accident or something that The Old Man had planned all along?"

"What difference does that make?"

"I'm not sure, but something about this has me thinking that there is more here than meets the eye, so to speak."

"I think you better get up here then. I'm not sure I'd know what you're looking for."

"Neither am I."

An hour or so later, I called a personal transport, and this time, I made sure it was one of my own and that I would have control. Everything checked out, so I jumped inside. D'Awlia had promised to rehearse with W'Lillad to make sure that he'd be able to reproduce the effect on cue. Everything would be ready for the trial. As I set the controls for the ship, I noticed that I was happy. For the first time in days I felt in control. I could prove that I had seen the truth.

Intermittently, I picked up flashes of images from the planet. D'Awlia was putting W'Lillad through his paces and making sure that he could reproduce the broadcast effect. I called D'Awlia on com and notified her that I was receiving the images. It happened once again. I saw D'Awlia blow me a kiss. I assumed it was meant for me and not W'Lillad. I decided not to be jealous.

At last, I felt that everything was going to work out.

But the euphoria was short lived. When I called to confirm my arrival aboard *Cincinnatus*, there was no answer. I checked the com, but it seemed to be operating fine. I called D'Awlia again to confirm it, and she registered that the signal was received 'loud and clear'. I tried to call the ship again. There was still no answer.

137

This is wrong. Someone should respond. Auto systems on the ship should pickup, at least.

I told D'Awlia that I suspected foul play.

"Do you think it's the same person who dropped you on the tower?"

"Maybe. There might have been some kind of accident. I won't know 'til I get up there."

"Be careful. We need you back here."

"Understood."

I approached the ship cautiously, hailing Claude and Zachary along the way, but there was still no answer. Finally, *Cincinnatus* was on the view screen. I circled the ship a couple of times, but I could find nothing unusual. I suspected a trap.

 I entered the airlock. This was the most dangerous part. If there was an ambush of some kind, this is where it would happen.

I parked the transport quickly and leapt as far into the airlock as I could, ignoring several sirens that rang close to my ears. I cycled the outer doors closed, waited a few minutes and then cycled them open again. That would take care of any foreign presence that might have been activated when I arrived. When the door cycled closed again, I shot the bolts on the hatch and sprang through the inner lock, even as it was still opening. It was unnecessary. My proximity sensors already relayed the information that the corridor was empty, but I was taking no chances. I took a cautious approach to the bridge. I heard only my footsteps. I searched for other signs of life, but there was nothing. No sound, no smell, no sign of a fight. Nothing.

I leapt through the door to the bridge in a crouch, but found once again that it was a futile act. I was hoping for a fight of some kind, but was met with a handwritten note propped in a corner of the control couch.

"Special Agent Shicker," it read. "So this is your ship? We need to talk. I'll be in touch. A friend."

For the first time in my life, I was worried for my family.

I tried to discern what had happened. There was nothing out of place. There were signs that Claude and Zachary were taken by surprise without a struggle. A half-drunk cup of tea at Claude's station – he was normally pristine with his utensils. An entertainment vid was stopped mid-frame on Zachary's bunk. He was less careful than Claude, but under the circumstances, it seemed to indicate an interruption.

"Computer, where are Claude and Zachary?"

"They are not aboard this ship."

"Thank you. When did they leave?"

"Indicated personnel departed zero minus two hours and fourteen minutes."

"Did they say where they were headed."

"There was no indication of destination."

"Has anyone else been on this ship in the last two hours and fourteen minutes?"

"Special Agent Shicker."

"Besides me, who else has been here in the last few hours – um, before I arrived?"

"Special Agent Shicker."

Maybe I wasn't being precise enough –

"It was a Special Agent Shicker that was here before myself that you are referring to, right?"

"Correct."

"Oh? Well. That's an unexpected development. What made you think it was me, er , Special Agent Shicker?"

"Logs indicate that Special Agent Shicker utilized personal codes to access ship's systems." *Damn. I'd been meaning to change those codes.*

"Did he take anything?"

"He downloaded flight information onto an external shipboard computer."

"Did he leave anything?" I suspected a booby trap of some kind.

"He recorded a manual message and left the contents on the bridge." The note.

"Anything else?"

"Negative."

"Where is Special Agent Shicker, now?"

"He is on the bridge." *That's me. At least he didn't change the access codes.*

I ran a scan of the system, but there was no sign of another ship about. No surprise. There were plenty of places to hide, or they could have folded into instell.

I checked the logs and filled in the gaps. Someone had discovered my access codes. Difficult, but not impossible for an accomplished hacker. They used it to track me to the Kozarian system, parked nearby. Dad and Claude probably noted the ship and sent some sort of a message, but it might have been intercepted or perhaps jammed. Then the intruder must have entered and abducted my family. I couldn't imagine why my family might have left on their own.

There was nothing for me to do except to wait to hear from the bastard and hope that I would get the chance to get my hands on him.

"Computer, send a priority message to The Old Man. Tell him that we have an emergency here. Tell him I'm without backup or support and if has any contacts on Kozar, he'd damned well better let me know! Wait! Change the message. Make it read: 'urgent emergency'. Set a security-coded message for return. Make it assessable only from my quarters on the planet."

I wouldn't get an answer for a few days, but if Claude and Zachary were gone then I needed help as soon as I could get it. I checked for any other abnormalities in the ship's systems. I found nothing out of place. I put in a call to the planet.

"How could they have vanished into empty space?" D'Awlia asked over the com.

"The easiest place to vanish into. There's so much of it."

"We need you back here! We need to demonstrate the optics tomorrow."

"I'll be back in time. I promise. But, I need to help them."

"What can we do?" she asked.

"Wait until the intruder makes contact. We'll see what he wants and try to get ready for him."

D'Awlia was deeply worried. "What if you're not back before tomorrow's session begins?"

"I will be. Somehow."

"I don't like this."

"Neither do I, but the only thing I can do is wait."

I didn't need to wait for long. Soon, ship's klaxons began to ring feverishly. Another ship had just bloomed onto scans.

Cincinnatus had limited armaments, so I had few options. I ordered weapons on line.

"Request denied."

"What?!"

"All security functions must be cleared by Special Agent Shicker."

"I am Special Agent Shicker."

"Negative. Annunciating party identified as unauthorized intruder."

"When did that happen?"

"Approximately zero minus forty seconds ago."

This was not good.

"Who identified me as an intruder?"

"Special Agent Shicker."

"Where is Special Agent Shicker, now?" I demanded.

"Special Agent Shicker is in corridor three between passenger lounge and command module."

Right behind me!

I turned quickly to see a tall man standing in the doorway leading to the passenger cabins. He sported a well-trimmed beard and mustache, a skin-tight electric blue ship suit and a phase inverter short gun with a cold power source. The last held most of my attention.

The stranger announced, "I have taken control".

"So, I see."

A short gun is a nasty weapon – a perfect sidearm for shipboard battles. Typically, it is poked through a cycling airlock and fired, neutralizing everything in front of it. It has a very short range, and its charge typically disintegrated before penetrating bulkheads. Its short range is redeemed by its ability to hit virtually everything in front of it, and depending on the strength of its charge, it could neutralize or kill anything in its path. It looked like an inverted funnel; its business-end a wide, six-centimeter, gold-plated ring.

"I have imposed my codes to override the ship's controls," he claimed. "Go ahead and make an order to the primary systems."

"Computer, target incoming ship and fire

immediately."

Nothing happened. The intruder laughed. "Nice try. And forget using the communicators. I've locked you out of that function, too."

"You seem to have everything under control."

"Yes. Unlike our last encounter, but you won't be running away this time. Or jumping off any balconies."

"And you won't be diving into any garbage heaps, either, I suppose."

His smile vanished. He was getting down to business. "You noticed my ship approaching. I waited until I spotted you leaving the surface and then charged up here to meet with you." I assumed that he somehow had tapped into my transport call requests. This was the second time he'd used it to get the jump on me.

"I should've checked the passenger area when I found your note. Stupid of me."

"You can't think of everything."

I took a wild shot. "I should have thought to leave a crew on board to greet you properly."

"They wouldn't have made a difference. I would have disposed of anyone I found on board. You might still survive if you behave yourself."

"If we're going to talk for a minute, perhaps I should brew us up some grog, huh?"

"Go ahead. We have a couple of minutes. I won't be having any. Speak clearly, I won't have you muttering any commands that might interrupt us."

I ordered up a drink. I had just learned two important facts. Dad and company weren't on board when the intruder arrived, and I still had access to low order commands.

"We won't be staying here long, so drink up."

I took a long swallow.

143

"What's the game plan, then?" I asked.

"In a couple minutes, my ship will be here. We go on board, I'll ask you a few questions and if you give me the correct answers then I may let you go. I may not, though, depending on how cooperative you are." I deduced the events of the past few hours. He came aboard the ship, utilizing my access codes. He boarded just ahead of me, intent on clearing the ship. Zachary and Claude either escaped before he arrived or are still hiding out somewhere. I hoped for the latter, although I didn't see much chance for it. He waited for his ship to approach before changing the codes, knowing that I would react and probably find him, which would have spoiled the day for one or both of us. Now, he expected me to walk willingly onto his vessel with promises that he MAY let me leave. I didn't like the odds.

Whatever else, however – he wanted me alive. I planned to use that to my advantage.

"What is all this about?"

"I'd rather not say. Too much depends on secrecy right now. No telling who may be listening."

That gave me an idea. If Claude and Zachary weren't captured, then they might be within com range. I couldn't use the com line, but he may not have shut down the data link.

CLAUDE! ZACHARY! RESPOND!

I could see the renegade ship approaching. I only had a couple of minutes, and there was no response from my father or my son.

"Finish that drink. The ship is docking."

We would be walking the length of the ship. I tried to think of some way to distract this man long enough to gain the upper hand, but I could only manipulate the ship's minor systems to turn the tables.

144

He jabbed the gun in my back, and I moved without hesitation in the direction of the airlock.

"You know, I'll be missed. I have an important appointment tomorrow."

"Tomorrow?" he chuckled. "That gives me five hours to ream your brain! Plenty of time...."

Oops! That left me just a few seconds to find away to get out of this man's grasp. Once I boarded his ship, it was all over.

CLAUDE! ZACHARY! RESPOND, PLEASE!

Nothing. *Who said you can always depend on family?*

We were moving through the narrow corridor leading to the airlock. Another thirty seconds and I was as good as dead.

COMPUTER, SHOW ME A LIST OF ALL FUNCTS I CAN ACCESS.

A menu flashed in front of me, thanks to the prote controls. A quick scan of the list made it clear that most were lounge and convenience features. I had been reduced to being a passenger on my own ship. I looked closer at the list.

Basic Medical Aid
Liquid and Solid Refreshment Dispensers
Sonic Cleansing Units
Audio Entertainment
Viewport Controls
Lighting Controls...

Lighting controls! I've got you now!

Timing was everything. The short gun would hit nearly everything within a 180-degree arc from the nozzle. I had to somehow be behind, or at least to the side to avoid being hit. A plan came to mind. I pictured the steps in my head. It might just work.

We were approaching the inner door of the airlock.

Good safety procedure mandated that the airlock doors were normally to be operated manually. When we were within a few steps, I sprang forward.

"I'll get the door – "

"Wait!"

As I expected, he thought I was setting up a trap. He jumped ahead to intercept me. I stopped short of the switch by a meter and stepped to the side. He rushed on past me.

COMPUTER, TURN OFF ALL LIGHTS.

I had the instruction all typed out and pressed the send command as he jumped past me. Proximity, subcon, and infrared were already on line, so I didn't lose track of him or the short gun as he cycled the door and the lights were extinguished.

It was totally dark for him. I saw perfectly well.

"What! Hey – !"

I grabbed his wrist with one hand and his elbow with the other, and then slammed his arm on my knee that was coming up hard. Something snapped as he spun toward me. He screamed in pain and managed to fire a charge, but I had been careful not be in front of the funnel. I was able to pry the weapon from his flimsy grasp. He bent over in pain as I positioned myself for a low g drop kick that sent him sprawling through the door. As I cycled the airlock closed again, I heard him order the computer to turn on emergency lighting, but it was too late for him. I sealed the door with manual safeties. Even the computer couldn't bypass them, so he wasn't going to come back in that way.

His only choice was to blast the ship to pieces. He might be mad enough to do it, but I hoped he wanted me alive bad enough that he would listen to logic and not fire on my ship. His own vessel was still attached, and I could tell that he was trying alternatives to get through the airlock. As long as he was doing that, I felt relatively safe. Airlocks are built to take the most abusive punishment imaginable, and as long as his ship was tethered to *Cincinnatus* there would be no fireworks between vessels.

When he stopped banging on the airlock, I waited for a new attack. I was trying in vain to hack the new access codes when I discovered his tactic. The oxygen alert sounded. He was going to suffocate me by leaking my lifeline into space. Normal procedure would call for me to access EVA oxygen in the airlock, but that was where the intruder was. I would have no choice but to submit to his demands. I didn't like that alternative.

I could have tried to use his short gun against him, but he was probably ready for that alternative. Maybe he had a phased shield. Whatever the case, I wasn't going back there. Instead, I headed for the passenger quarters. The air was already getting thin, and I was starting to get light headed.

"Special Agent Shicker. Perhaps you've noticed that the air is getting a little stale. I've turned off your oxygen replenishment, and I am venting the ship's air into space. It'll take just a few minutes, so you better get back to my ship where we can talk."

I found what I was looking for. A compact oxygen supply. It was meant to be used in an oxygen emergency, but only to get the passengers to the airlock where they could reach a supplemental air supply. There was only about a five minutes supply in the canister. I put it over my face and dug up as many others as I could find. There were only six more canisters. I considered putting myself into stasis, but that was risky with less than an hour to work with.

"You hurt me back there, so I can't promise that I won't hurt you, but I will vow to let you live. Coming back here is the only chance you've got."

I knew my only chance was to hack those codes. I returned to the bridge, pleading with the computer to shut off the oxygen drain and return control of the ship to me, but the reeking machine wouldn't listen. I didn't know the name of my assailant, so I didn't even know where to begin. I ran random numbers and letters, but it would have taken a year or so to check all the possibilities.

"I only need one little piece of information. That's all. When I'm satisfied, I'll let you go. I swear, and I'm a man of my word," the comline broadcast.

I had gone through three of the remaining canisters when I realized the futility of the situation. I pried open a control panel and tried to find the oxygen control. There had to be a manual release.

"Frankly, I don't know how you managed to hang on this long. Sensors show you still moving around, though. You are a very resourceful individual."

I dug through the wires, tubes, pipes trying to determine which, if any, might help me. There was nothing that I could see, but I was getting desperate. I was on the last canister. My hands were fumbling as I pulled a red tube line as far into the room as I could manage. It gave me only a few centimeters of slack.

"Time is short, Special Agent Shicker. For both of us. We don't want you to do anything rash. I'm sure you don't want us to act rashly either, do you?"

This must be it, I thought of the red tube. If not, then I was in trouble. I had just tossed away the last oxygen canister.

I cut through the flexible pipe. A low K frozen gas sprayed close to my face. It would have blinded me if I wasn't already blind. I fell to the floor in pain. My face burned with the cold. Safety valves closed and shutoff the spray. I began to gasp for breath. It was hopeless.

"Time is up, Special Agent Shicker. You've made a huge mistake."

I considered giving in to the intruder, but I would never make it to the airlock in time. My head was reeling.

I found myself thinking, *One of these days, I've gotta find out who this guy is.*

I came to in blackness. I knew this wasn't heaven. Dad was here. I heard his voice.

Zzzkkktt-wwhhrr!

I brought the beasties on line even though I already had a monster headache.

"There you are," Claude pronounced. "See, I told you he'd revive." There was a medical compress on my face and a supplemental oxygen tube in my throat. I carefully removed both and fell back into the bed in which I was sprawled. I sighed in relief. I had just survived another close one.

"This son of yours is a genius!" Dad declared as my son checked my pulse. "He saved our butts! Yours, too!"

"Not really. I just recognized a dangerous situation," he replied.

"No shad! That renegade ship unfolded, and then it came right for us! It was bristling with weapons, so we didn't stand a chance against it. And if we lost our shields, we'd be sitting ducks–"

149

"Blind sitting ducks!" Claude corrected.

"Claude saw that we would have been cornered in the ship, so we dropped everything and left on our landing transport. We hid out while he checked out our ship. It was just one man, and he boarded as easy as you please. He must've been disappointed that he didn't find you. He left right away, and we followed the shadhead to the other side of the planet. We lost him there and tried to get hold of you. D'Awlia said that you were looking for us, but we couldn't raise you, so we came back here to the ship."

Claude jumped in. It was nice to see that the two of them were getting along better. "We found the ship docked to ours, and thus we determined that you were in trouble. There wasn't much that we could do, so we tried to stay out of sight. Then we heard him on our com asking you to surrender. We didn't know what else to do, so I used my override codes to cancel yours. He lost control of our ship then. We beamed up weapons and shields, and he got scared and left. I guess he figured that you were on the edge of being suicidal, and he didn't want to die with you. Oh, we also brought the oxygen back on line, you'll be pleased to note. Now, we are reconfiguring our flight path so that we won't be so easy to find next time."

"Hopefully, we won't be here long enough for him to get another fix on us," I said.

Dad revealed a more urgent need, "D'Awlia has been calling for you. We told her that you were okay, but she wants you back on Kozar."

"What time is it?" I asked.

"0920."

"Shad! I'm late. I've got to go!"

"We found some interesting information on the

soneds while you were 'resting'."

"No time!"

"Stay calm, Dad," comforted Claude. "We can discuss it over the com. See if it helps you. Take the landing craft this time. It's safer. He won't be able to trace it."

I rushed into the courtroom as E'Lowa was saying, "D'Rab. Enough of this Human intervention! They have nothing but lies to offer. They aren't even here to back up their absurd testimony – "

The was a rustling through the gallery as I hurried through the door in a pant. I made sure I caught E'Lowa's sight. *Now I've got you.*

I apologized for being late. *This is not a good beginning. The demonstration had better work.*

"We are giving you a chance to prove your testimony. I will have to say that your tardiness makes your testimony more suspect than ever."

"Your Honor, I was detained. Unavoidably. If you ask your people, though, you will find that I have not been near the optics or any of the important exhibits. I haven't even been on the planet for the last eight standard hours."

"I hope you are prepared to demonstrate this sight of yours. We have wasted enough time this morning."

"Yes, Your Honor. Again, I'm sorry."

I signaled to D'Awlia to begin. She asked that the optics be brought into the courtroom. W'Lillad entered through another door with P'Clellan's soneds in hand and whispered something to the judge. D'Rab said something to him in return and ordered that he sit near him at the judge's table. W'Lillad removed his optics.

Okay, beasties. Time to be useful.

"Your Honor. E'Lowa and others here would dispute what I saw. I couldn't explain what was happening or why it was happening. Until I discovered that there was something special about P'Clellan's optics. It was designed originally to transmit the vision it collected. I suppose some engineer thought that there might be reason to record the sight from the optics for future history. Perhaps they did it just because it could be done. Whatever the reason, they eventually scrapped that function and removed the micro switch which activated it."

I called W'Lillad to stand. He placed the P'Clellan's soneds over his eyes.

"Kozarians have many mannerisms with their hair. Sometimes it seems like your manes have a life of their own –"

"We don't normally talk about it," D'Rab responded, blushing, "Especially in a public hearing." There was a general titter throughout the courtroom.

"I'm sorry, but in this case, the act of brushing hair actually had an unusual effect. It caused the villi to make contact with one or both of the broken leads and activated the broadcast mechanism. Watch what happens. Mr. W'Lillad will tell you that I have not had any physical contact with optics in any way –"

I cued W'Lillad. He brushed his hair in an imposing way and then followed through with the relaxed gesture. I waited for the beasties to react, ready to switch to proximity sensors.

Nothing happened.

"Well?"

"I'm sorry, Your Honor," I laughed with unease. "These things never work the first time."

152

"Or EVER, if you are covering for a lie," claimed E'Lowa. There was scattered laughter in the gallery.

"Let's try again." *Come on, Beasties!*

I pointed to W'Lillad again, and he performed the essential gestures. There was a tense moment of waiting that seemed to last for hours. I half-expected to fail.

Zzzzkkktt-Wwhhrrr!

It happened. I tried to contain my excitement and let the protes take control. I slowly brought up proximity sensors so that I would not trip over my own feet in front of this audience.

"Well?" asked D'Rab.

I've got you, E'Lowa. Now, you'll pay.

"It's working."

"What do you see?"

The pixels phased in. I saw myself standing in front of a crowd of Kozarians. I gripped the edge of the chair. It was still difficult dealing with the vertigo that accompanied the broadcast vision.

"I see the courtroom."

"Of course he sees the courtroom! Are we really going to put up with this?"

"Give him a chance, E'Lowa. Proceed with the demonstration."

"I would like to ask some people to stand behind me, out of my view, but where W'Lillad can see them." I stepped into the corner while D'Rab selected three people. One at a time, I correctly named K'Croft, Colin, and then D'Rab himself.

"Parlor tricks! This means nothing." E'Lowa was beginning to sweat. He was shifting in his chair. His hair was doing an interesting dance of its own. "There are a thousand ways to stage the same effects."

153

He was correct, of course. I could think of several means that didn't even require high-tech equipment.

"What kind of test would you suggest?"

I could see the wheels turn behind E'Lowa's optics. He looked at me askance. I couldn't tell if he was considering a fair test or one that would be impossible to accomplish.

"Alright. I know. If you are willing."

"Go ahead. Put me through your crucible."

"W'Lillad, come with me. You, –" he pointed at me with the force of an accusation, "describe what you see when we leave the room.

"Fair enough."

E'Lowa left with W'Lillad and a court official who would take notes during the test. Another stenographer took notes on what I said. The door closed with a heavy slam. The real test was underway.

"You may begin at any time," D'Rab directed.

"I see the hallway. No surprise there, I suppose. He is leading me, um W'Lillad into the elevator. E'Lowa is saying something. I don't know what – I can't read lips." There was a brief buzz of laughter.

"The doors are open now. We're in the hallway again. I can't tell which one. We turned to the right. Oh, he is looking at a picture. A landscape. A mountain and a low building with columns, I think."

"The tomb of T'Damen! Outside of P'Clellan's room!"

"Silence!" ordered D'Rab.

There were shushes around the gallery and a muted "Sorry."

"They are entering a room. P'Clellan's room. I recognize it. E'Lowa is holding something up. A statuette of an animal. It is a – hard to tell – looks like a squid, but what's the Kozarian equivalent – shaped like this." I grabbed a pencil from the table in front of me as D'Awlia thrust a piece of paper into my hand. I sketched the figure with multiple tentacles that I saw. I couldn't see what I was drawing, so I hoped that I had made a fair representation. The page was taken from me when I finished. I heard it rustle in D'Rab's hand a moment later.

"We are moving into the office now. We are going to the desk. E'Lowa is calling me over. We are going behind the desk." As he was moving around, W'Lillad looked up briefly. There it was again. A glimpse of the last thing that P'Clellan saw. The angle was a little different, but there it was. The door that E'Lowa raced through as he fled the room. The green vase was gone, but otherwise –

The vase?

"Mr. Shicker?"

"Um, sorry. He's at the desk. Just a moment, everything is black. He is shielding the optics with something. Okay. E'Lowa's writing something now. On some parchment on the desk. I can't read it. It's written in Kozarian. Uh, hold on. I'll try to write it. I guess that's what he wants."

I tried to reproduce the blocky script. It was dark, as if something was obstructing the view. They were only letting enough light through to write the characters, but W'Lillad was giving me a long look at the page, so I had plenty of time to copy it down. I didn't have the chance to see what I was scrawling, though, so I was worried that I may not be getting it right. As I was finishing, the image suddenly blanked out. I hoped that W'Lillad had removed the soneds and that something hadn't gone wrong.

155

I also prayed that E'Lowa hadn't pulled a trick of some kind. I had a sudden feeling of dread. Why had I allowed E'Lowa to conduct the test? If the Kozarian could kill a man to get his way, then he couldn't be trusted to conduct a fair test. *He must've duped me somehow. How could I have been so stupid?*

My beastie sight was coming back on line. I turned to D'Awlia. I was frightened. "I think he cheated!" I whispered urgently.

"What?" she replied. "Ssshh. There coming back in."

I couldn't keep still. This was going to be bad. D'Awlia was moved by my nervousness. She tried to calm me. "You did wonderfully. You have nothing to worry about." *How could she say that?* She seemed so confident. She even smiled. What did she know that allowed her to stay so calm?

The room was abuzz when the three inquisitors returned. W'Lillad was all smiles, and E'Lowa stoically returned to his chair while the stenographer brought his notes to the judge. D'Rab compared the two sets of notes and then called the court to order.

"We, in this court, heard Mr. Shicker describe the little journey which was just taken to P'Clellan's rooms. He accurately described the objects that were subject to W'Lillad's concentration. The painting and the Rigerdabel were accurately described, but, as E'Lowa has said, there are many ways to reproduce the same effects as repeating what was seen through the optics. Therefore, I will negate any of the sights described in the first few minutes of the journey as being irrelevant to the proof of the testimony Mr. Shicker has given. There is just no way to be assured that we are not being fooled in some way. I'm sorry, but we cannot trust this

156

part of the test completely, so I am ruling it as being insignificant."

There was a murmur in the courtroom. E'Lowa smiled in satisfaction that he was proved partially correct.

"There is only one thing which Mr. Shicker described which can be held as refutable. I will rely on that description alone to prove his testimony. E'Lowa, please confirm that this is the note that you wrote."

E'Lowa rose and went to the judge's table. He looked at the page that D'Rab held and nodded, then he returned to his chair. I couldn't read his expression.

"I assume you took precautions against any tampering during this portion of the test?"

"Yes, W'Lillad and I are the only ones who could have seen what I wrote. I shielded the page from all possible viewing angles except through the optics."

"This is it, correct?" D'Rab held the note up to the court. It was written in broad enough strokes that even those in the rear row could read what it said. The crowd reacted. A chuckle began to spring from divergent points of the rooms. The laughter spread. I waited in silence. I couldn't recall from what I saw if I had copied the inscription correctly. I had no idea what the Kozarian letters spelled out. I had no choice but to wait.

E'Lowa continued, "I took specific action against other humans manipulating the test, as well."

"What further precautions did you take to ensure that there was no tampering?"

"I wrote the words upside down."

The stenographer piped in, "Yes. I noted that Mr. Shicker wrote the words upside down when he copied them."

E'Lowa went pale at that revelation, his mane going suddenly limp.

The judge held the two pages side by side. "This is the note which Mr. Shicker wrote. As you see, they are nearly identical." There was applause scattered through out the room, as if a show had just concluded. I didn't know how to react to it.

D'Rab finished his remarks. "I am satisfied and willing to give Mr. Shicker's testimony due consideration."

He adjourned the court. I was relieved. I had passed the test. The room began to empty with a smattering of chuckles throughout the departing crowd. I received several pats on the back.

"What did the note say?" I asked D'Awlia when she finally released me from a protracted bear-hug.

"It said: 'Due to the lack of a decent education, humans cannot read this.'" I shook my head in shock. E'Lowa had just put his own head in the noose.

I looked at E'Lowa who was still seated at his place and discovered that his sightless eyes were locked on mine. He had removed his soneds and tossed them onto the table in front of him. His assistants were speaking urgently to him, but he ignored them and stared at me in mute accusation, as if I had somehow maneuvered him into incriminating himself.

Then I noticed something disturbing about his eyes. Something different from the murderer whom I saw kill the Kozarian leader. E'Lowa's eyes were green.

They were the wrong color.

Chapter Twelve

"There are a dozen possibilities," D'Awlia assured me. "You could have remembered it wrong."

"I didn't remember it wrong, I know that," I said.

"He could be wearing tinted lenses. Maybe he's doing it now to make you recant your testimony. Or he could have worn them when he murdered P'Clellan. Are you having doubts?"

"No. Just raising questions."

"Let me see if I can make you raise something else, instead."

She didn't quite succeed in completely distracting my attention, but it did prove to be a pleasant diversion. We were celebrating, of course. The court, based in large part on my testimony, cleared K'Mack, and was now considering leveling charges against E'Lowa. The government was in a temporary state of upheaval as factions were realigned and a new chain of command was established. After E'Lowa, who was dealing with issues of his own, K'Mack was the logical replacement for P'Clellan. It seemed as if Humanity had won its objectives. The Old Man would be pleased. And, he owed me a favor.

Colin prepared a lengthy report on the situation.

We had been scheduled to leave the next day, but departure had been postponed again. I was asked to stay until charges were filed against E'Lowa. I found myself anxious to leave. I sought certain information for a personal mission of my own, but the new complications would delay the pursuit for a few more days. I hoped that whatever timeline Trace was on, our further delay wouldn't prove costly to her.

Her welfare became my overriding concern and began to infiltrate my relationship with D'Awlia. She could sense that I was distracted, and although she accepted it on the surface, deep down there were more ardent feelings that were beginning to cause friction.

I was also concerned about the inconsistencies that I noticed between the physical evidence and my testimony. All could be explained, but D'Awlia tended to pass over the details a little too flippantly for my taste. I liked to have every detail fit neatly into place. Especially when what I said may sentence a man to his death.

"What about the vase?" I pondered.

"The what?"

"I clearly remember that the vase was next to do the door as E'Lowa ran out."

"It must've broken after P'Clellan died. Maybe it was teetering."

"But K'Mack had shards of it on his clothing –"

"That's it then. He must've bumped it when he discovered the body and it broke."

"But witnesses agree. There was a crash – and then a scream."

"Maybe E'Lowa broke something else and later K'Mack broke the vase."

"Witnesses only heard one crash."

160

"There are ways of breaking a vase without making a crash."

"I suppose." I stated, but I could tell she wasn't interested in pursuing the subject at length. Still, I went on. "What about the angle of attack?"

D'Awlia let out an impatient breath. "We've been through this. He was on his knees, or E'Lowa climbed onto something."

"A blind attacker climbing onto a chair? I don't think so."

"Okay then," concluded an exasperated D'Awlia. "P'Clellan was on his knees."

"And what about the eyes? I know I saw blue."

"Maybe you need to recalibrate your beast-thingies."

"If so, then the vase should have been blue instead of green, also."

"Or perhaps you just remembered it wrong."

That was her final argument to support all of the inconsistencies. But I didn't like being wrong in the present or the past. Not in a case like that. Our discussion ended. The answers would have to come from somewhere else.

An hour or so later, I was called to see Colin. She requested that I meet with her in a room on one of the upper floors of the building.

It must have been a rec area for the prisoners at one time. There were monitoring devices of various sorts in the hall and devices of mysterious function in the rooms that I hoped were exercise stimulators and not elaborate torture implements. Colin assured me that they were, but I didn't know how she purported to know. The floor smelled of musty powder, and it seemed as if this part of the building was seldom used. The thick patina

161

of settled dust also supported my conclusion. This was not a regularly traversed area. The window treatment made this even more more apparent. They were covered with thick, mildewed, insulated drapes to block the adverse effects of the sun. At the far end of the hall, we turned into an expansive room that glittered with stainless steel mesh that covered the walls like wallpaper. Colin closed the door behind me after peeking down the corridor one last time as if to make sure that we weren't followed.

"Your 'friend', D'Awlia, told me about this place. I knew the Kozarians had them, but I didn't know they still worked."

"A hologenerator? I wouldn't expect one on a sightless world."

"The first Humans here came across them. They must've been out of service since the flares began. Here's the real trick, though." She removed a crystal sphere from the pouch she had been carrying and placed it in the center of the room. Next, she touched a control near the door. A moment later, a transparent white box shimmered in front of us. It was large enough to step inside. Colin entered and beckoned to me to join her. I did.

Stepping inside was like entering another world. The dimensions of the room were impossible as it would have extended through the walls of the governmental building. I knew this place. It was The Old Man's Sanctum.

My beastie sight told me that this was an illusion, of course. A holographic image. A good one, but not impossible to see through, and occasionally, the image stuttered. I turned around and saw the paraplegic guards standing outside of The Inner Sanctum. They

162

didn't move, but then, they never did.

The guarded door swung open and through it marched The Old Man himself!

I turned to Colin aghast. "Is this 'real time'? Can he see us?"

She nodded in affirmation.

"This is impossible. How is this accomplished? He is over three light years away."

"I don't know. He provided us with the sphere and told us how to make it work. It took several tries, but–"

The Old Man waved to us and came near. He was semi-transparent, but otherwise convincingly real.

"Hello, Kit. Glad you are well."

"Thank you. You can hear me okay?"

There was a slight delay, but given the distance – "Yes. Fine. You can go, Colin. Kit will return the device to you when we're through."

She nodded and left. This was going to be a private talk between The Old Man and me.

"You gave me quite a scare a few days back. I returned your message. You can just delete it when it arrives. Sensitive information, you know." He didn't explain why he could not have returned my urgent message for backup through this communication vehicle instead of instell com, but I knew it was not that important to him to answer my request for back-up. He would just say that he had faith that I would pull through despite the adversity.

"You look good, Old Man. Where's the cane?" Every conversation with The Old Man MUST include a brief discussion of his health.

"I died a few days after you left. The new clone can walk without it. My new afflictions are of a different sort. A few are more difficult than others, of

163

course. I'm afraid I've lost the faculties of my taste buds. Outwardly, not too inconvenient, but it spoils my enjoyment of Clarice's famous nasi goreng." He indicated the medicine bottle on his belt. "At least I can't taste this swill anymore."

"I'm sad for you."

"Don't be! I'm fine, and you've done me a great service on Kozar. All Humanity will thank you."

"The right man is going to be punished. I just did what I had to do."

"Of course you did, of course you did. But I consider it a personal favor, and I'd like to reward you for it."

"You know what I want in return. We've discussed it."

"Yes, and I've got good news. I have discovered where your wife is."

"She's not my 'wife', and where is she?"

He forged ahead with his tale. He was not one to be sidetracked when he had a juicy story to tell. "We checked the logs of the flight she was on. She got on the ship. We have her on vid, but she never got off. Impossible on a folding ship."

"I know that much of it."

"Yes, but you don't know the rest of it." He looked at me, annoyed for interrupting. "We closely studied the vid of the ship loading. No one else got off before it left, except the loading crew. They all checked out fine, however. They brought supplies in with large crates, unloaded the crates then took them off again. We suspect that she was in one of the unloaded crates."

"Suspect doesn't sound too definite to me," I argued.

He continued as if I hadn't said a thing. "Our

suspicions were confirmed when we traced the loading crew. One of them is a man we suspect of having a lucrative smuggling trade: one Neville Bevington."

I knew that name from the distant past. Very distant past. "The name is familiar, somehow."

"It should be. He was once set to marry your wife. He shunned Trace –" He looked at me for a reaction. I gave none. "– or she shunned him when it was learned that she was pregnant–" Again he paused for my reaction, and again I didn't show a thing. "– with your child."

He was playing with me, but I didn't have the patience for games. "So, now he wants her back?"

"Possibly. Or he wants revenge."

"Revenge?" I asked "Why do you think that?"

"Because he is also after you," he claimed with the hint of a smile. "Neville Bevington is the human renegade who has been chasing you around Kozar."

Chapter Thirteen

"So all this time, we've been close to the man we needed to find," Zachary was pacing the deck like an angry lion. "Why didn't The Old Man tell us that! We would have captured him. Shad, we would have had Trace back by now."

I speculated, "He was afraid that if he had told us that Neville had Trace, then we would have left Kozar and not helped win the negotiations."

"He told you that?"

"No, but it makes sense – using The Old Man's logic." I had already thought this through. "If we achieved our objective without him then he would have nothing to hold over us."

"He leaves nothing to chance," said Claude. "He designs plans within plans, plots within plots, contingencies within contingencies."

"Claude, do you remember Neville?" I asked. "He was part of your colony for awhile."

"I have a faint memory of him. He left our group of refugees once we found transport off Bogolich."

"Do you recall anything about him?"

"Not really. I was very young at the time."

Zachary was still pacing. "Well, at least it gives us

a course of action the next time we meet the shadhead!"

Claude touched a control and brought up a 3-d holo display of the soneds. "We discovered something else about those optics. Apparently their design predates your vision implants."

"What?" That was a surprise.

"I know. I assumed that they based the design of the optics on your sight, but it was the other way around."

"The beasties come from the soneds? No wonder the images the optics generate are so primitive – and so limited. I thought that the engineers just didn't want to show the Kozarians everything they could see. So, I actually owe my sight to Kozar and its enigmatic sun."

"So it seems."

"When did their sun go nova?" I asked Claude who was proving to be an excellent researcher.

"It is tough to say, relatively speaking. I mean, I can give you a standard year, but you want a year based on your timeline, right?"

"Right."

"Let me work on it."

"In the meantime, Computer, set a course for that Orphan probe. I want a look at it."

"Coordinates unknown," stated the mechanical voice of the ship's control.

"Follow the readout signals and trace their source."

"Acknowledged."

Zachary and I left the bridge and entered the galley. He drank a thick ale, and I satisfied myself with cold ice tea. We sat in silence while Zachary played with his drink. Something was on his mind, and I waited for it to surface.

"We didn't start very well," he blurted. "I'm sorry

about that."

"You mean on Shoorulia?"

"No, I mean the beginning. Us."

Oh, the beginning....

The beginning was difficult. I was leading a happy life as an Orphan. Advancements with proximity sensors meant that my life as an interstellar pilot would not be limited. In fact, I felt sorry for sighted people. I couldn't see the advantage of sight no matter how hard other Orphans tried to convince me.

One day, a White Coat approached me with the chance to see. The technology was there. I qualified for cybernetic enhancement, something that was difficult to do with the restrictive biomech laws that were in place. At first I turned them down, but The Old Man had a special interest in my case. He knew my father. I didn't, so I offered to become his agent if they granted me a chance to meet him. It was arranged, but first I was to get my sight.

It took a year of intense training to use my new vision. At first, I was taught basic visual sight which was tied into the proximity computer. I was given mnemic programs that taught me color, shapes, and sizes and tied them to memories, both real and programmed. I spent days strapped into place while new colors were flashed into view. Shapes were formed and unformed before my mind's eye. Things grew from microscopic to gigantic. It was almost like learning a new language. And then it would start all over again.

Just as I got used to one enhancement, they added another. I spent months in the hospital, sometimes close to death, as new beasties were dropped into my eyes. The Old Man came through for me when I most needed it, and I emerged a healthy, new man.

Next, I was granted a visit with my father.

"Hello, son?" Dad said upon entering my cubicle. My quarters were barely a room, but it was all I needed for the time. My first assignment was due to begin the next day. Zachary was barely two years older than me at the time.

"Dad?" I gave him a hug. I felt that I needed to, but it was uncomfortable and the embrace ended quickly.

"They seem to have taken good care of you," he said, "and you can see now. That's great!"

"Yea. I guess so."

He quickly explored the few contents of the cube until he ran out of interest. Then, he began to shuffle nervously from side to side. "So – "

"So – "

"Sorry," he said. "I don't know what to do. You're too old to take fishing."

"What? They have a zoo in your Hub?"

"No," he said, "it's an old Earth custom. You wouldn't know about it."

"Guess not."

"So – ." There was an uncomfortable pause. "What do you see?"

"It's hard to describe. A lot, I guess."

"Suppose so. I know The Old Man has big reeking plans for you."

"I guess. Listen. He has been good to me, and I've been thinking – since I'm your son, maybe I should ask him to move me to your Generation."

He began to shake his head.

"They allow families, right? We could be together,

169

and maybe work the same crew ships. I know that Mom is not around and your ships are slower, but...."

His head continued to shake.

"No, I couldn't handle that," Zachary said. "We're almost the same age. And your Generation needs pilots. It is a great opportunity for you. I'd tie you down."

"You mean, I would tie YOU down."

He dropped his head and studied the floor as he spoke. "Yes. I guess that's it."

I looked away, disappointed. The Orphans were as good a family as I could ever hope for, but somehow, it wasn't enough. I thought I would feel tears, but none came.

"Listen," Zachary said, "I know they have a gravcourt here. I feel like getting some of the herring out of my joints. Wanna try a round or two?"

"No. I'm supposed to rest. The beasties are still taking their toll."

"The beasties? Oh. Well then get your rest. I'll, um, be in touch, okay?"

"Sure."

He left, turning back once more as if he had something else to say. Then he was gone. The next time I saw him was in a bar on Shoorulia.

"No," I said. "That didn't go well for either of us."

"I just wanted to say that I was proud of you. The way you are now. I mean, a father is supposed to say things like that, but I mean it. I would want my son to grow up to be just like you are. No different at all. I doubt if I would have done any better, in fact, I probably would have done worse."

"Don't sell yourself short."

He started to say something else and then just tipped his glass to me and smiled. It was good to see. "In fact, I hope to be just like you when I get to be your age," he said.

"Thanks, Dad." I chuckled softly and returned the toast. Then I had a serious thought. There was something important I had been meaning to ask him, but there never seemed to be a good moment to raise the question. "Dad, why am I here?"

"You mean, like, your 'purpose in life'?"

"No. What was Mom like? What happened to her? Why did you leave?"

He studied the bottom of his glass as if he were looking for a lost charm. Looking up, he said with a sigh, "It is more complicated than you can imagine. I'll spell it out as best I can I guess. I'm not sure myself of everything that happened. Or why."

I waited silently.

"The Old Man set up the First Generation. I don't know if at first he planned to make more Generations or if he suddenly discovered that he needed to fill some gaps in our long distance runs. Too many pilots were going out on long runs and not returning for decades. He needed a new Generation. He went to the only source that he knew he could access at the time, his Orphans. Remember that at the time, only real parentless orphans were chosen to join – the missions were considered too dangerous. But then, we started to marry and have families and it seemed like we could stay together. The Old Man approached a number of us and said that he wanted to create a new Generation. He was recruiting some colonists, but he wanted to take some of the traits which the First Generation exhibited and build it into the Second Generation."

"So he started a breeding program?"

"Basically. He told us that there were no obligations. In fact, he didn't want us to be obliged. We would create the kids and then leave. Basically, new Orphans with living parents. We didn't feel good about it, so he backed off on that demand a little bit, but he did make it clear that there would be limited contact between Generations."

"Who did he choose to do this?"

"Well, that's the strange part. The pairings didn't make sense. He had some kind of genetic data, though. I 'married' a nice young woman that I barely knew, Ruthie was her name, and next thing I knew, she was pregnant. I was then given a long assignment, and you were born while I was away. I heard that Ruthie died in childbirth. Not unusual for us Orphans, I guess. In fact, a number of children and mothers from the program died within the first year. Others were handicapped, like you. I guess, you can't force these reeking things. Anyway, I felt sorry for her, and I truly missed her. What could I do? I knew that you were in good hands, though. Orphans take care of their own. Shad, I suppose I should have demanded to be with you, but I was given another long mission, and it seemed better just to go."

I took in the information and considered it in silence for a moment. "Thanks. That explains a lot."

"We have this time together, now. Let's make the most of it."

"Right, Dad."

Claude's voice sounded from the intercom, "I have the probe on scan. We only have a few minutes this close to the sun, so you'd better hurry."

Dad and I hustled to the bridge. The view screen

was filled with the undulating colors of the Kozarian sun. It was less spectacular than the colorful effect that the electromagnetic storm had on the atmosphere of Kozar, but unusual enough that we paused momentarily to take in the spectacle.

There was a tiny, dark spot set against the colorful background of the nova. Claude informed us that our shields were strong enough to last for seven full minutes. That was time for only one pass by before we were chased back to a distant stellar orbit.

"What are we looking for?" Claude asked.

"Anything unusual."

We recorded every reading from our scans as we watched the visual display enlarge. Zachary increased the magnification.

The probe was a tubular-shaped device that was caught in a close orbit. It was equipped with the usual protections against the radiation from the stellar furnace. It had a triple thick titanium hull and a regenerating EM shield. Two antenna arrays adorned the object, one pointed toward the sun, and one pointed away. The arrays were each transceivers and could both simultaneously send and receive super-EM signals.

Zachary spotted a discrepancy. "What's that attachment?" he asked.

"It's got a parasite!" said Claude.

I increased the magnification. "I guess I'd call that unusual."

"Not human."

I double-checked the recorders. We would need to go over the readings in detail once we returned to Kozar. "It is broadcasting on a direct narrow beam straight to Shoorulia."

"It's a reeking Shoorulian bug!" Zachary exclaimed.

"Interesting. The question is whether The Old Man knows it's here."

"Hard to say." I was thinking out loud. "I don't think he would cooperate with the Shoorulians to that extent."

Zachary tracked our thinking. "So, the Shoorulians found this human probe and tapped it in order to keep track of the nova?"

"Easier than building one of their own," Claude stated. "They analyze the Human surveillance, and if the nova ceases for a significant period of time, then they move in."

"Then let's burn the reeking thing off."

"No. That may be a cue for them to attack," my son said. "Even a brief lapse of data might catch their attention."

Dad had difficulty sitting still when he discovered alien intrusions. He asked, "So, what should we do?"

It was an interesting development, but it changed little of significance, unless The Old Man was part of the Shoorulian tap somehow. "Nothing. We'll let the Kozarians know that it's there. When they have rebuilt their defenses, they can destroy the whole damned probe."

We tracked past the probe quickly and silently. We had little time to make more than a passing observance. The shields were working hard to keep the radiation at bay and needed distance from the star in order to replenish themselves.

"Why are there transceivers on both ends of the probe?" Dad asked.

"It is an old design," revealed Claude. "Some

would say 'ancient'. It's from your epoch, Granddad."

"I hate hearing the words 'ancient' and 'epoch' being associated with my timeline."

"Nevertheless, it's old. I suppose it grants a certain measure of redundancy for reliability. Unnecessary – it's worked all this time – but you can never tell with proximity stellar monitoring. It also gives you another advantage. It can give you a constant, almost moment-by-moment surveillance of the nova's activity. You don't have to switch back and forth between receiving and sending to get the data you want."

"That seems unusual to me," I said. "Is it critical to monitor this phenomenon so closely?"

"It depends on what you're monitoring it for."

"And it has been in operation for how long?"

"In standard years, we're talking centuries. By the way, I ran the calculations against your timeline," reported Claude. "This star went nova the year you were born. Happy Birthday, Dad!"

A coincidence? "Not a present that I would ask for."

I must have reacted sharply, because my father looked at me askance. "What is it?" he asked.

"Nothing. Just a lot of little things. I'll just be happy to leave Kozar, I guess."

"I concur," said Claude.

"Make it unanimous."

"I am slated to testify against E'Lowa tomorrow. Then we can find out what Neville has done with Trace."

We moved away from the probe, and thus the nova. Our approach took us around the far side of the sun. Kozar was a long three hours away, and shields wouldn't begin to recharge until we entered orbit and rerouted the engines to power them.

Unexpectedly, the computer blurted, "Emergency."

To our horror, a blip appeared on our scans.

"It's him!" called my son. "It's gotta be Neville! I'm setting our course to intercept him."

I paused. We couldn't put up much a fight. We had our backs to the nova that was draining our shields, and so retreat would be impossible. He had the better weapons, and one or two hits and our defenses would fail, blinding two thirds of my crew.

But I was eager to get my hands on this nuisance. Although I had encountered him twice before and come out on top, I was still unsatisfied. I had done little more than run from the man, and I was used to standing and fighting to a resolution. Somehow, we would find a way to beat him.

"Okay, let's get him," I ordered.

"Wait!" Dad interrupted. "Think! We can avoid him if we change course, now."

I shook myself. *Was this my father speaking?* He was famous for rushing into battles with little more than a laz and a prayer. Was he now backing away from a fight?

"We can't meet him now. We're too weak," he said.

My son pleaded, "But if we miss this chance, we may never see him again."

"I don't want him to get away," I agreed. "He's got Trace."

"You don't know if she's with him, and there's a good chance that he has her stashed away somewhere far away from here. If we destroy him we'll never find her. I don't see how we could cripple him enough to get control of that ship."

176

"We've got to try!" said Claude.

The blip was larger now. On full mag, we could begin to make out the silhouette of our enemy's ship, barbed with armaments. If we had spotted him, it was a sure bet that he had spotted us as well. We had only a couple of minutes before evasion would be impossible.

"Maybe Zack's right," I said.

"No," Claude argued. "We are lucky that The Old Man told us about him, otherwise, we might have left this system without confronting him."

"And why do you think The Old Man first urged us to avoid confrontation at all cost? Do you think he was concerned for our safety then and not now?" Dad argued. "What has changed? Think about it. Maybe he was afraid that Kit might discover Neville's connection with your mother. But maybe he was really afraid that Kit might be decommissioned and wouldn't complete his mission. Now that the treaty is about to be put into place, maybe Kit is expendable. Or maybe – ," He wasn't speaking to either Claude or me now, but to himself. I could see the wheels turning behind Zachary's eyes. He had experienced enough of The Old Man's manipulations to know that there was always a reason behind every move he made. " Maybe, he prefers Kit dead – now that his mission is fulfilled." He turned suddenly to me. "You say that now you are having doubts. Perhaps there is something to that. If there is something more to the reeking murder than what you saw, then Humanity might be better off with you out of the way. Shad, you are the only one who would know that something is amiss." He bolted for the manual controls, but Claude intercepted him. "We've go to change course, now!"

"No! We've got to attack!" Claude exclaimed.

177

I thought about it for a second. Dad was right. I could think of no tactic that would even get us close to Neville, let alone give us an advantage. Plus, the renegade was itching for a fight, and I could no longer be sure that he wanted me alive.

"He's right. Let's avoid contact. We'll catch him later."

"What!" screamed my son. "How can you say that? We'll lose him if we don't get him now."

"No. Not now. It'll have to be later."

"Mom's life is at stake! Sure, you've had your fun dallying on the planet with that Kozarian woman. You probably don't care about Mother anymore, but I do! We've got to get her now!"

Claude struck a distant chord. For the past few weeks, I had put aside my real reason for coming to Kozar, but recently, guilt had begun to surface. The guilt was bundled with another realization. That I still loved the woman I met on a spaceship years ago. The woman who bore and raised my child on her own and who had apparently never lost faith in me. I owed her something.

But that was an emotional response, and there was no room for emotion right now. If we didn't survive the encounter with Neville, then we wouldn't be doing Trace any favor.

"I do love Trace, but we can do nothing for her now. Take evasive action."

The computer responded quickly, overriding Claude's trajectory orders, and our ship swerved heavily inside the orbit of the innermost planet. Our scanners picked up a torpedo heading in our direction, but it was fired from too great a distance away. The sun's gravity snared it and reeled it in far from our location. Little jinks of the controls, and we had effectively avoided Neville's ship. At least, he didn't show up on our scans.

Shields were already beginning to recharge as we entered a new orbit around Kozar. Dad sighed a breath of relief when it was clear that we were out of danger. "Thank God that's over," he said.

I looked into my son's face and saw nothing there but hatred. "Is it?" I asked.

Chapter Fourteen

I returned to my quarters on Kozar. D'Awlia was there, but I obliquely acknowledged her, despite her attempts to gain my full attention. I also ignored the insistent blinking on the com terminal. I knew it was the message from The Old Man that had finally arrived, but I couldn't find the concentration to attend to it. I had too much on my mind between my guilt of not trying to recapture Trace, the alienation of my son, and the anxiety I was feeling in regards to my "eyewitness" testimony. I felt I couldn't do much to resolve the first two, so I decided to settle the third. I left D'Awlia in my room and like the proverbial criminal, I returned to the scene of the crime.

Outside of P'Clellan's room, I discovered that the door had been locked. I was considering forcing the entrance when I heard a door open nearby. I turned to find K'Croft emerging from K'Mack's rooms. He spotted me and approached quickly.

"Haunting scene, huh?" He must have divined my purpose for being there. "I can imagine that it is tough to get out of your head."

"Yes. You could say that."

"Here. I can unlock it for you."

He pressed a hidden key of some sort and the door swung open. We entered the outer office. It was still as I remembered it from my last visit, but it was the inner office that held most of my interest.

"I want to thank you for what you did for Kozar," he said as we moved slowly through the room. I wanted to note the minute details, or perhaps I was procrastinating. Mostly, I didn't want to rush things. "Aside from providing the optics, you have done an admirable thing."

"How's that?"

"Testifying for K'Mack."

"You mean testifying against E'Lowa."

"You upheld the truth, that's the important thing. You didn't need to. It might have been easier to ignore the situation and just leave Kozar to fare for itself. Kozarians admire actions such as yours."

"I just did what I thought was right."

"That's what I mean," he said. "We admire people who act on their convictions. In fact, there are many who even admire E'Lowa for what he did, even if it was for the wrong reason."

"I'm afraid, I couldn't abide that." I turned to face K'Croft before entering the inner office. He was giving me new insight on the Kozarian way of thinking which I hadn't been able to fathom to that point. Kozarians seemed eager to follow anyone who had a strong opinion, even if that opinion didn't make much sense.

"Of course, but you have to understand our past. We have always asserted our independence. For ages we were tied to the Shoorulians. It was the most determined of our people who made it possible to leave the planet we shared. We have always followed the most resolute of our people. Compromise has been a dead-end for us."

"I don't see how it works. How can you make progress without some form of compromise?"

"If you know that your opponent will be uncompromising, will do anything to win, and prevent your opinions from being heard, then you think twice before asserting your opinion. If you are sure of your opinion, then you need to speak out loud and long to have a chance of being noticed. That's the way it always was with the Shoorulians, and I suppose it carried over into our politics. We've always had violent factions holding contrary positions. It is our leader's role to choose between differing sentiments which are always diametrically opposed."

"And are your leaders always assassinated to drive through a decision?"

"Not often."

"But sometimes?"

"Sometimes."

"Sorry. It seems counterproductive to me."

"It all depends on your point of view."

We entered the inner office, and I tried to recreate P'Clellan's dying point of view. I actually lay down on the floor and peered toward the door. It was nearly the same that I remembered, but I was sure that there was a vase next to the exit. Now, there was just an empty pillared table. I got back to my feet and tried to recall the final attack. I stood on my toes to reproduce the angle of P'Clellan's sight. I tried a number of different heights, but I couldn't remember well enough to match the view I had seen.

"What's the matter? Having doubts?" K'Croft asked. "Of course you are. When so much depends on a memory, you can never be sure if what you remember is accurate."

"Except I am sure. That's the problem."

"Well, time has a way of coloring memories. Things are not always exactly the way you remember them. It's too bad we can't just replay the images in our head."

"Like a vid or a holo-sim?"

K'Croft shrugged in answer. I had a moment of inspiration. I'm not sure why, but I asked K'Croft to let me try his optics.

"Maybe if I looked through a Kozarian's prosthesis I would have better recall," I explained.

He handed his soneds to me without hesitation, but I didn't put them on.

"I thought it conflicted with your cybernetic sight."

"I just want to see if it will help me recall what I saw that night. There, how do I look." I still held the optics in my hand, so I knew from his response when he looked over at me that he was completely blind. I also discovered something surprising. K'Croft had eyes of a color I had seen only once before – in P'Clellan's dying vision. His eyes were the same unlikely blue as E'Lowa's angry gaze during that deadly attack.

I returned the optics to K'Croft and went back to my quarters. There were just too many coincidences and unexplained inconsistencies. It no longer made sense, and I could no longer trust my memory. I needed help, and I turned to the only source that might help me explain what was going on: The Old Man.

His message was still on the com when I entered.

"Satisfied, yet?" D'Awlia inquired. "You really should put it behind you."

"I can't," I said. "I testify tomorrow."

"Just say what you said before, and you'll be okay."

"I can't."

I activated the com. His message was a reply to the emergency communiqué I had sent days before when I feared that my crew was lost, and I was alone. I asked The Old Man to indicate if he had contacts on Kozar. If he did have agents on this planet, they might be able to help me work out what actually happened – or what I had actually witnessed. I suspected that Colin might be more than she seemed. Or perhaps The Old Man had been in touch with K'Mack, or maybe even K'Croft.

But the message was more than I had bargained for.

Kit, Your message concerned me greatly. Get whatever assistance you can! I have only one contact on Kozar who may be of limited use. Her name is DAwlia. We need that treaty! Good luck! T.O.M.

D'Awlia?!

I was stunned but more than my beastie sight was coming into focus.

I turned to face her. D'Awlia was seated on the bed across the room. I began to walk towards her slowly. It was all coming together. It began to make sense. The angle of the knife blow, the shards of green glass, the color of E'Lowa's eyes.

"My darling? What's wrong?"

It never happened. The murder I witnessed never happened.

E'Lowa was innocent. K'Mack stabbed P'Clellan to death after all.

I was set up to be an eyewitness to convict E'Lowa. By D'Awlia, a woman I trusted.

I was a couple of paces from her when I confronted D'Awlia. "How long has this been going on?"

Her mane made a sudden transformation. It suddenly came alive like a sack full of worms. She knew that she had been caught.

She tried to deny it, but her calm beauty belied the desperation expressed in her voice. "Darling?"

"I just received a message that you've been in contact with The Old Man. I want to know how long have you been working for him?"

"Kit! Please!" she pleaded desperately.

I reached for her. She shielded her face, but I didn't strike her. Instead I grabbed her writhing hair at the nape of her neck. Kozarian villi are highly sensitive tactile organs. Grabbing it was akin to grabbing a male human by the testicles. She expelled a sudden gasp, but I had her full attention.

"How long?" I asked again.

"Kit," she said, "It doesn't need to change anything!"

"Since before P'Clellan made his decision?"

"No one will know!"

"Since the last days of the negotiations?"

"Earth will have its treaty. Kozar will have its sight."

"Since before the negotiations started?!"

"You can stay here with me. We can live together – build a new home. A new planet!"

"Since before I arrived?"

She nodded in affirmation.

I released her and let her drop to the bed. She put her head in her arms, then looked up at me. "Don't you see?" she asked me. "It was worth killing for! It would be worth dying for!"

"Tell me what The Old Man said."

She turned from me. "I got a message from him

after the optics were supplied to us," she said. "He said he needed someone to make sure that negotiations would go through. He would sweeten the pot for all of Kozar if it did. He said that a person with special sight would be arriving. He said that in an emergency you could be made to see certain things. He told us how to activate the transmitter."

"Whose idea was it stage the murder?"

"It wasn't mine alone."

"The Old Man?"

"No. K'Mack dreamed it up. And K'Croft."

"But the suggestion was there. From The Old Man."

"I don't think so, but maybe it was," she started to cry. "If it was then it was very subtle."

Plans within plans, plots within plots, contingencies within contingencies....

"Who else knows about this?"

"No one."

"Tell me how you did it. Start at the beginning."

She felt impelled. This at last was the truth. She'd lied to me before, and I believed every word without question. I knew that she would be honest, now.

"We were given the diagrams of the prototypes before we got the optics themselves. The Old Man contacted our faction and pointed out that there was once an image projector attached where you saw it. The receivers were not sent, however, but someone in the human party would be able to see the images if we had an emergency or needed to have something seen. He may have said 'witnessed', I don't remember. That's what gave us the idea that if the treaty didn't work out, then we could turn things to our advantage. He showed us how to activate the image projectors remotely. I think K'Croft mentioned assassination, and K'Mack thought of a more subtle way of getting both E'Lowa and P'Clellan out of the way."

"Go on."

"I was given the task of accompanying the 'observer'. That was before I fell in love with you."

"Stop! Don't even use that word!"

There were a few moments of tears, and I had to coax her, none too gently, to continue.

She resumed, "I was to monitor you closely and determine the best times to send the images. We planned to do it first in the airlock, of course. Then when K'Mack met with P'Clellan and we could somewhat control what was seen. Finally, we staged the murder after K'Mack got the bad news."

"How?"

"From the holographic image chamber. It made setting the scene easier, but we were prepared to stage the whole thing from one of the unused offices. The blood just seemed more real from the holographs."

"So, after you learned that P'Clellan was going to expel the humans, K'Mack told everyone that he could find that the treaty was on. Then he waited until E'Lowa left, and he killed your leader, knocking over the vase in the process."

"We were actually proud of the performance. Everything worked perfectly."

"Not everything," I said.

"We planned for as many possibilities as we could. The performance was actually delayed a few days when E'Lowa refused to wear his optics. We had to reprogram the holograph. Then you kept leaving the building. Everything needed to be timed perfectly, so we had to wait to the last minute when we knew where everyone would be – E'Lowa, P'Clellan, and you –"

"So you staged the murder that I witnessed, but there were discrepancies."

"P'Clellan knocked over the vase. That wasn't part of the program. K'Croft played the role of E'Lowa in our rehearsals, so we misjudged the angle of the attack. We also never saw the color of E'Lowa's eyes. He was always wearing optics when we had ours on, so we had to guess and based it on the color of K'Croft's eyes, too."

"So, K'Mack had just enough time to reposition the body before the guards found him."

"Then we had to convince you that it was real. That was easier than we expected, but we also needed to prove that the optics could transmit P'Clellan's sight. We thought that was going to be easy, but you kept missing the signals I was sending. I must've brushed my hair back a hundred times before you noticed."

She smiled and sniffed back the tears, trying to convince me that I should find the humor to laugh at her frustration. She even brushed her hair in that famous way, trying to encourage me. It didn't work.

Her nostrils flared. Desperation turned to anger. She finally unleashed the fury of her Kozarian determination. "We thought you were one of us. We thought you agreed with our purpose – to give sight to our world. We almost told you our plans and let you in on our mission."

"I wouldn't have gone along with it."

"You don't have any idea what it is like! A whole world without a future! Without hope! How dare you judge what we have done!"

"You forget, I am blind myself."

"We made it work! We accomplished our mission.

And whether you like it or not, you have come too far to turn back now! You are one of us!"

"You may have fooled me into helping you, but never mistake me as being one of you. I was raised better than that."

I turned my back on her, deep in thought. I had a difficult decision to make.

Could I play along? Pretend that I still believed the lies I witnessed? Send the wrong man to whatever fate the Kozarians used to punish murderers?

No, I couldn't. Even if Humanity gained control of this sector, it wasn't worth living with this lie. The Old Man must've assumed that I would play along. That's why he waited until now to tell me who his informant was. He thought that it was too late to change the course of events.

"Kit!" she called to me as I reached the door.

I left the room without saying another word.

Damage control. *How can I salvage the situation and still bring about the treaty?* I couldn't see a way. And I couldn't be silent.

I was a fool.

"Who has evidence to present against E'Lowa for the murder of P'Clellan?"

All eyes in the courtroom turned to me. They were all here. Both factions of the Humanity negotiations: E'Lowa, K'Mack, K'Croft, D'Awlia.

D'Awlia.

I could feel all of their stares, as if I was being hit with something tangible, something heavy. It could have been easy. Just readmit my "eyewitness" testimony. Then I would be through. They would all be happy – all but E'Lowa and his people. Kozarians

189

would have their soneds, the planet would regain its sight, The Old Man would have his treaty, and Humanity would have access to this vital piece of space. I could leave the planet, find Trace, and live happily-ever-after.

The silence in the courtroom was deafening. I almost stood. It should have been easy. Stand, say a few words, and then leave. But that would be giving away too much of myself. I looked directly at the judge, but I said nothing.

There was no other evidence but mine to hear. The judge asked the next inevitable question. "Who has evidence to present in behalf of E'Lowa."

I could have stayed silent. The Human faction might still have won out in the end. But I was slowly pulling myself to my feet, as if I was carrying a great weight. This too should have been easy, but I found that I had to tear the words from my mouth like a man trying to pull his heart from his throat. I heard D'Awlia's gasping moan as I reached my full height.

"Your honor," I began. "I've made a terrible mistake."

Chapter Fifteen

"The Old Man wants to see you immediately," I was informed on returning to the Orphanage.

"I know. I'll try to fit it in my schedule."

The trip out of Kozar was as uncomfortable as any I had ever experienced. We were asked to leave immediately after I finished delivering my testimony that implicated K'Mack and his faction in the conspiracy to kill P'Clellan. We left as soon as all the optics had been rounded up. Colin was clearly out of sorts. "Why couldn't you just keep quiet!" was all that she said to me. I expected the statement to be accompanied by a slap in the face, but she somehow restrained herself. She chose to make the return voyage in stasis, giving me the only good news I had for the entire trip.

Claude was unhappy about leaving Kozar and Neville behind. He wanted to make one more attempt to capture the renegade.

"He's sure to follow us back to The Hub," I explained. "We'll make contact with him there. Tell him that I'll give him anything he wants for Trace's safe return."

That set my son back a little. "Anything?"

I just nodded in reply. We scarcely exchanged another word for the entire return journey.

Dad was unusually silent. He seemed to be watching me closely. I wasn't sure why.

We unfolded close to The Hub and docked uneventfully. I half expected to be met by an armada of warships, but The Old Man didn't punish people like that. I had no illusions. I knew he had heard the news from Kozar long before we arrived.

My first stop in The Hub was to visit Walt in the labs. I found him in the regen chamber staring up at The Old Men suspended in the tanks. It looked as if he expected them to give him the answer to a mystery. I sniffled and caught a sterile odor of iodine. The air was cold, and I wrapped my ship suit tighter around me to keep out the chill. Poor Walt spent most of his time in the subzero environment.

"You waiting for them to speak to you?" I asked.

"I'm waiting for them to die. We are losing more of them than ever before."

"Any chance of him dying out in the next day or two."

"Not likely. We have too many in reserve."

"Pity."

He gave me a look out of the corner of his eye, and then directed me into his lab. "I think the entire system needs to be recalibrated. We've made so many copies of copies that sixty percent of them never make enough neural connections to keep them alive for more than a few hours. We need new blood. Literally"

"But that's illegal."

"I know. We aren't allowed to clone anyone who isn't The Old Man, but he's just not a good specimen anymore. It takes us weeks to successfully grow one with all the knowledge of the present ones. It should only take a few days for most adults. And of course, each has to be equipped with alpha wave receivers – in case they do happen to survive, they have to be up to date on what The Old Man knows."

"We wouldn't want The Old Man to lose out on the latest fashion trends, would we?"

He gave me a circumspect look and began his usual examination. Walt took blood and other body fluids.

"Thanks," he said.

"Enjoy," I replied.

The regular physical tests were run. He retrieved the scoop and inserted it into my tear duct shunt. I winced with pain.

"This isn't good," he said when he examined the test result. "You have a low count on nearly everything. You need to give the protes a chance to rest! They have lives, too, you know! They have to eat and rest and reproduce! If you keep abusing them this way, they'll rebel!"

"And then what?"

"Then," he smiled in reply, "You come see me, and I'll fix you up again. That's my job."

"Sorry, but the little beasties have been busy."

"I've heard. The Old Man wants to see you right away, you know."

"I know. I'm going to see him tomorrow, I guess."

"Well, I better set you up then. This'll probably hurt a little bit, but you'll be able to see The Old Man when you see The Old Man. When you're through with him, come back and I'll check everything over before you head out again."

"You are too kind, Walt."

In a few minutes, I was fully equipped and ready to meet with The Old Man. Physically ready, anyway. When Walt had everything he needed, I rose from the examination table. He clasped my hand hard as I set to leave the labs.

"Take care of yourself," he said and maintained his grip. He looked deep into my eyes as if to transmit an unspoken thought. I understood.

"I will. You too, Walt."

I left and checked in at the gravcourt. Sara was there as usual, and she challenged me to a one-on-one match. She knocked me around quite a bit. I didn't mind.

Needless to say, I lost. It was a feeling that I was getting used to.

After the game, she shook my hand. "The Old Man is looking for you," she informed me.

"Oh? I guess I better see what he wants."

But I wasn't ready, yet.

I returned to my quarters and commed Zachary. Claude was in the Orphanage somewhere, but I hadn't seen him.

"I've gotten a message from Neville. He's been right on our tail, and he's looking for you."

"Did you give him my message?"

"Yes. The Shadhead was thrilled to hear it. He seems happy to give up Trace. Are you sure you want to do this?"

"I have no choice."

"Your life will be in danger."

"I'm used to it by now."

"We'll back you up, son."

"I know. I'm going to meet the Old Man tomorrow."

"We'll watch for the fireworks."

"I'm hoping he'll be reasonable."

"Yes. Well, he is the most reasonable man I know," Dad paused momentarily. "He's reasonable to a fault."

"His Achilles heel?"

"If he has one, that would be it."

I wanted the conversation to continue for a minute or two longer. I was not sure why. Finally, I had to let it end. I signed off and went to bed, knowing that I wouldn't sleep.

I was about to confront the most powerful human in the galaxy.

It was going to be a big day.

Chapter Sixteen

"You've been a naughty boy, Kit."

I couldn't move. The paraplegic guards held me securely in the chair. I would be forced to talk it out face to face with The Old Man.

I went to the Sanctum as soon as I awoke to the light of the artificial morning. There would be no avoiding it. The Old Man would have it out with me sooner or later, so I might as well get it over with. Perhaps he would see the value of doing the right thing, despite the cost.

Clarice made a gruff and thorough search, but she didn't take everything. Only the weapons. She asked for the gravbelt, but I told her that unless she wanted us to hold the meeting on the ceiling, then she'd better let me keep it. She did. I began to believe that I might just survive the upcoming meeting.

But, The Old Man was not as cordial as I had hoped. His guards grabbed me before I took two steps into the room and dragged me to a chair opposite the elderly ruler. I began to look for weaknesses in the guards with scans tuned to their most sensitive. I didn't expect to find an obvious frailty.

The Old Man waited for me to cease struggling

before he started to speak. His ancient age was still apparent. The elasticity of his face was gone forever. His head was barely more than a skull, the transparent skin barely concealing the veins and cartilage. Yet, his spirit did not suffer. He sat patiently. His face shown with a freshness that his predecessor had lost, and he seemed to have boundless energy. I wondered what medicines he might be taking. "Okay. Let him go. He won't cause any trouble, will you, son?"

"No guarantees," I answered.

"Always the fighter. I could always count on you for that. Such a human trait."

"I admit, I'm still human – " I looked around at the other occupants of the room. " – maybe the only one here."

The Old Man chuckled at that. "I may not seem completely Human to you. I've had to rise above that. Humans used to fight over matter, and over space – mere lines on a map. I have eliminated the need for that. I don't care about 'things' anymore. Only 'time'."

"I don't understand. I thought that you wanted to keep the Human colonies expanding outward."

"No. I'm more concerned about the hourglass."

"The hourglass?"

"A metaphor. An hourglass shows the passage of time by the number of grains of sand that trickle through a narrow glass funnel. Now, I control the sand. I am in the position to examine each grain of time before I allow it to fall through the channel. Each grain contains everything–every person, every object, every planet, every moment. And they all must pass by me. I control them all."

"That is a huge responsibility."

"A lesser man couldn't handle it." He took a casual

swig from his medicine bottle.

"Are you sure that you are 'handling it'?"

"I was –" I could sense with heat readouts that his blood was boiling. It corresponded with sudden flush of color in his cheeks. I was afraid that he might explode. " – Until you messed things up on Kozar! That is the one grain which slipped through my fingers!"

"I did what I thought was right."

"I wanted – expected – you to do what was best!"

"You underestimated me."

"I overestimated you! I thought you would rise above your personal morals and do what was correct for your people."

"That makes no sense."

The Old Man seemed to regain his composure. I could tell that he had already thought out a new course. For humanity, and for me. "It does, even if you don't see it. But it doesn't matter, because you are going back to set things right."

"I don't think so."

"You will. You'll see. Everyone does what I want in the end. I have ways of making people see the light."

"In other words, you force them to do what you want."

"Not what I want. What is best for Humanity."

"And who decides what is best for Humanity?"

"I do."

"And what qualifies you for that job?"

The Old Man swept his arms around the room, I suppose to indicate the universe, but I only saw his four walls. "My boy, I see everything that happens in Human space. I am in the best position to evaluate all the possibilities."

"Why not let people decide for themselves what is best for them."

"Ha! Self-determination is a nice idea, but it is futile. With so many people going in different directions, pursuing different goals, none but a few get what they want. Even fewer get what is important. I am providing direction for all of Humankind. Let me give you an example. Ever hear of Threstantia?"

"No. I've been out of touch."

"It is a planet which has an upper crust that is made of diamonds. Not just an isolated area but the entire planet. I gave the colony there the job of mining the jewels. We needed the resource for our technological advancement. They refused. They wanted to lead a more pastoral life. They wanted to preserve the environment. I remember that they were especially fond of a native flying lizard that they said would die from our mining processes."

"What did you do?"

"Simple. I gave them their self-determination. They wanted to live off the land; I gave them the opportunity. I stopped sending transports."

"An embargo."

"Self-determination. It's what they wanted. They ended up starving. In the end, they even ate their loveable, little, flying skinks." He closed his eyes as if he had suffered through the experience. "Poor, miserable people. I think there are still some of the colonists living in the hinterlands."

"And the diamonds?"

"Oh, I got them. When the first colony died out, I sent in a new one to occupy and mine the planet."

"How many in the original colony?"

"Fifty thousand or so. They were just starting up."

I shook my head. Fifty thousand dead. This was how he had set up the colonies. Each specialized in a certain set of tasks that supported the other colonies, and all were connected by his Orphans. The Old Man would never allow the colonies to become self-sufficient. That would bring about the end of his influence. Humans would stay dependent on him and his Orphans forever.

"You're a tyrant," I muttered to myself.

"Tyrant! How dare you use that word! You don't know what is involved. You don't know how hard I try to make things right for all of Humanity. I weigh all the options carefully. Don't you see? I'll do anything to advance Humanity. Everyone is better off."

"Kozar is better off without us. Why don't we let them fend for themselves."

"This isn't about Kozarians. This is about Humanity. Kozar was an obstacle that I had under control. Now, you've spoiled it all, but I'm not going back to square one."

"Square one?" *The beginning. Alpha.* The Old man was on a roll, so I decided to keep him talking. I still had a lot of unanswered questions. "And what exactly was square one? When did you start manipulating events there?"

"Longer than you know. Longer than you've guessed."

Longer than I've guessed? I assumed that The Old Man had his hands in the stew since before the design of the prototype soneds. He said that he designed my sight himself, so he must've designed the optics. He designed them to transmit images to my beastie sight, but did his involvement on Kozar go back before that?

The Kozar sun went nova after the first human

contact, but not long after. My god! Could he do such thing. Technologically, he probably had the ability, but did he have the depravity to perform such an act?

I will do anything to advance Humanity.

"Oh my god! You did it! You made their sun go nova!"

He turned his back to me. A silent answer, but one that left no doubt.

"Do you realize what you did?! How many millions died as a result? How many more suffered – are suffering still? That was an evil, inhumane deed."

The Old Man turned suddenly at that. "InHumane? Listen to you! You don't know what you're saying. I did nothing against Humanity. I helped our species. We needed to get into that space, they kept us out, and I found a way to get us there. That's all. I saved Human lives – Kozarian lives, too. Do you know what a war would have cost?"

"You've got to set it right! Reverse the effect of the nova. You've got to."

"No I don't, and I won't. You are so concerned for Kozarian life, but if the sun stops acting up then the Shoorulians will move in. You think that the loss of life was bad before, how do you think it will be when they move in on the blind Kozarians? It is regrettable, but I did what was necessary."

"We could have left them alone."

"Again, you aren't seeing the big picture. You don't know what they were like when we first met them. We couldn't leave them alone and advance beyond them with them at our flanks. A conflict would have exploded on us sooner or later. You didn't see them at their most potent. Eventually, there would have been a costly confrontation."

"I can't accept that there wasn't another way."

"It was the only way, and it was a relatively peaceful answer. And you were part of the solution. At least you were meant to be until you turned on your own people."

I had a sudden sick feeling. Something he had just said opened possible pasts and purposes that I never dared explore before.

I was part of the solution.

This manipulation goes back longer than you know. Longer than you've guessed.

The Kozarians were encountered before I was born. The optics were designed before I was born. He made the star go nova. Before I was born? No. After. Just after.

Oh my God!

"I am part of this, aren't I?" I asked, thinking out loud. "You paired Zachary and my mother for a reason, didn't you? You had the genetic data. You didn't want to fill the Orphan ranks with 'adventurous offspring'. You wanted a child to be born without sight – a particular defect for which you had already developed the cure. As soon as you had a child with the properly deficient eyes – one that could be legally equipped with cybernetic sight – then you created the nova and blinded a planet. You could afford the risk. You finally had what you had been waiting for – a child that would be raised as an Orphan outside of parental control. One that would be in-grained with a certain moral code. One that would be manipulated to see on a planet of the blind. One that would witness a murder that was never committed." I shook my head in disbelief.

"Could you really have been so far sighted?" I

wondered aloud. "You CREATED me to give false witness against your Kozarian enemies."

Plans within plans. Plots within plots. Contingencies within contingencies.

"I plan for everything. Almost everything. I never supposed you would sacrifice yourself and your race for your principles."

"Then you don't know me very well."

"Frankly, I am a little disappointed. You should be pleased. I've just given you a remarkable gift. Most people ask themselves 'Why am I here?' They never learn their purpose in life. You've just learned yours. Happy? Too bad that you've screwed it up so bad! You were supposed to settle the Kozarian situation, but instead you muddled it up. So many millions dead because you were born." The Old Man looked at me through the corner of one eye as if to distract me from what he was really looking at. "There is only one way to set it right. I'll show you how. You've got to go back –"

"No! I won't be a part of this anymore!"

" – It can still work out. They trust you now. You'll need to eliminate some of our enemies. I can help you identify them and choose the proper timing and method –."

"NO!!!"

I tried to stand but was immediately pushed back into my chair. It was jarring, but I gained invaluable data regarding the speed of The Old Man's cybernetic guards.

The Old Man threw up his hands in frustration. "You obnoxious fool! You can't know the importance of the situation on Kozar. You can't see the repercussions that events have set in motion. You can't

203

see the future implications. It is too large for you to see with your narrow vision."

"I don't like what I've seen."

"That is what I'm saying. You can't see far enough into the future or the past to know that what I'm doing is necessary."

This manipulation had to stop. Too many lives were at stake. Too many lives were ruined. The Old Man had too much blood on his hands, and he wasn't finished. He was the worst kind of tyrant – one who believed that he was doing good; that sending millions to die would be justified in the end. As imperfect as self-determination was, it was better than that. The Old Man had to be stopped.

Sonar found a weakness in the guards. Not a great one, but the only one that I could take advantage of. A stress point in the axillary joint under the arm. I double-checked with X-Ray and other forms of deepsight. Their metallic joints clearly showed through soft flesh. My implanted computer ran the numbers. Even with cable-reinforced muscle, the axillary connection was poorly braced. With the proper angle and strength of strike.... I marked each one with subcon and waited for an opportunity.

"I see what you've done," I said. "Maybe I can't see the future, but there is too much evil in the present. Perhaps the hereafter will correct the current evil, but we shouldn't wait to see if that comes to pass. Maybe that is too shortsighted. I don't know. I can only act on what I see. And my eyes – eyes you gave me – show me that everything you've done is wrong. Wrong!"

He sighed in exasperation. The Old Man actually put his arm around me and whispered in my ear. "There is a book on that table which I read often," he revealed. "An old Earth tome, <u>The Holy Bible</u>. There is a passage in it – " He laid his hand lightly over my eyes. The guards tightened their guard ever so slightly. "– It says, 'If thine eye offends thee, then pluck it out.'"

I let the phrase sink in for a moment. He was waiting for a reaction, so I gave him one. One that took him and the paraguards by surprise. I swung my fist straight out from my shoulder, but not at The Old Man. Instead, I slogged one of the guard's stress points with a well-timed, well-aimed blow. He was fast and nearly blocked the strike, but I was fast, too, and hyper-tuned to the subcon marker which pinpointed the exact spot complete with trace marks, trajectory projections and a hundred other readouts making it possible to hit the obscured and moving target.

My fist nearly shattered as I struck next to his armpit, but it worked. The guard's entire right arm tore from its socket with a thick ripping sound and a short splash of blood. It landed on the floor with a metallic clank.

I leapt back toward the outer door as the three stared at the arm that flopped from side to side with a life of its own. But Clarice came through the doorway with one of my own lazguns before I could reach the exit. It was blazing with heat, and I was sure that she was adept with lethal instruments, so I immediately reconsidered that route to safety. I did an about face and ran back toward the guards and the only other egress which offered an escape. The Inner Sanctum.

The Old Man fell back in terror, but the guards, even the one armed one, braced themselves for my attack. I reacted quickly, dialed the gravbelt low and vaulted over the heads of the cybernetic sentries as a laz shot scored my back. They snatched at my ankles, but subcon once again came to my rescue, and I twisted just in time, dialing the belt to the heaviest setting as I hit the exit. It splintered, and I was on the other side in the most influential room in the galaxy.

I wasn't able to enjoy the visit for long. Before I could pick myself off the floor, I was lifted up and thrown like a sack of bones onto the table. I was immediately immobilized. A firm hold was placed on my legs and another on my neck. I looked up from the large round table and into the face of The Old Man. Several of them.

These were his clones, each ruling a different faction of Human existence. The only apparent differences were slight and indicative of the handicaps imposed by the inability of the cloning technique to make solid neural connections: one of The Old Men wore an eye patch, another was in a wheelchair, one had both arms in a modified sling, and another had a face that sagged from numbness. They all stared in dumb surprise, and each was flanked by at least one cybernetic watchman. I thanked the beasties for giving me the chance to see this sight, and I started to laugh.

Pressure on my back constricted my breath, forcing me to reluctantly stop my hilarity.

"This is the man I've been telling you about!" announced The Old Man with whom I was familiar. He was crunching through the remnants of the door I had just crashed in.

"He's the one who acquired Kozar for Humanity?" asked an Old Man whom I couldn't see.

"And the one who gave it back again?" asked The Old Man with the patch.

"The same. I'm afraid that he'll have to be reprogrammed."

"Let him up," said the one in the wheel chair. "He can do no more harm."

"What do you have to say for yourself?" asked Patch in disappointment.

Suddenly the scene turned sour. It wasn't funny anymore. This was the man who had control over all humanity, who made life and death decisions on his own whimsical view of possible futures. And no matter which way I turned, I saw the same man – with different physical afflictions, but the same sick values. The sight was more than I could bear.

"If thine eye offends thee, then pluck it out."

I could do better than that.

"Alpha –", I began.

"What does he mean? The beginning? We have done too much to start over –"

" – Omega – " I could stop at anytime and the sequence would be broken. Or there were a half a dozen words that would abort the countdown. But I knew I wouldn't use them.

"The end? But there is no end. Time goes on."

" – Infinity – "

"Yes. There is no end."

I'd heard that The Old Man's paraplegic sentries had some form of ESP. Maybe they did. They seemed to sense that something was amiss and began to push their way toward me. I reached around the nearest Old Man and pulled him close to me in an embrace that would last forever.

" – Amen!"

"The last words of a prayer?"

"What are you saying?"

The Old Man in my arms looked at me amazed. He/they suddenly realized that something critical had

207

happened. His face froze in surprise.

It was the last thing I ever saw.

The kamikaze implant ripped us apart in a blaze of light and pain.

Chapter Seventeen

Blackness.
I saw blackness.
I felt blackness.
I smelled blackness.
I heard blackness.
I tasted blackness.
I was awake. I was asleep. There was no difference.

Chapter Eighteen

There was a flash of sensation. Strong arms took hold of me. I heard my father speak to someone in the distance.

Dad, I'm so glad to hear your voice.

I felt a rush of cold air. A shock ran through my body. I was wrapped in something warm and carried to a ground transport. I was placed in a fleece-lined basket.

"He'll be alright. He's still coming to."

Walt! How are you, old buddy?

"Let's disconnect the others."

"Go ahead. Half of them are dead already."

"Stand back. We're gonna bust things up a bit."

"Hey!" Walt shouted. "Keep the laz pointed at me! If anyone is watching, I wanna make sure they know that I didn't have anything to do with this."

There were a series of crashes and a muffled explosion.

"That glass receptacle up there that's dripping into the tanks? Better take that out, too. That fluid is almost impossible to replace."

There was a crash and a splash.

"That ought to do it," Walt stated.

"What are you going to do now?" It was Claude who asked.

My dear son! How wonderful that you are here for me!

"I think I'll retire to somewhere warm," Walt sniffled.

I found that I was crying. Real tears. I hadn't experienced that my entire adult life. They were tears of joy.

I was giddy for sometime, having experienced the strange euphoria that accompanied rebirth from a cloning tank. Walt, on his own initiative, used my latest blood sample for my regeneration. He grew them to adulthood for me using the pretext that he was "recalibrating" the clone tanks. He had implanted an alpha wave transmitter with the beasties to send my last thoughts to my clone while I visited The Old Man. Clarice found the usual implants, but missed the newest addition. It must've been covered by the protes. When the explosion ripped apart the Inner Sanctum, Walt contacted my father and let him in on our little secret. I was saved.

My body was like new. But I was blind. Totally. I didn't even have the basic auditory sensors to help me get around. The beasties were not part of the body that was cloned and so they were not reproduced. But, I knew how to get along without them and tried not to miss them.

It was not my intention when I visited The Old Man to commit a spectacular suicide, but sometimes you have to take advantage of situations when they present themselves.

The Human world was left in shambles. All but

three of The Old Men died in the explosion, and one of those died of an old fashioned heart attack shortly afterward. A determined witch-hunt was quickly organized to find those responsible for the rulers' deaths. I was correctly considered dead, so I had little to worry about. Claude and Zachary, however, were being sought; especially after the raid on the cloning chambers eliminated the reserve supply of Old Men. We fled The Hub and would have quickly folded to a distant system, but we had an important rendezvous to make first.

Neville Bevington was waiting for us at an appointed spot not far from The Hub.

"He has promised to turn over Trace, and he also says he'll let you live," Claude said to me, but he was clearly worried. "Do you believe him?"

"Doesn't matter. Death doesn't scare me anymore. I've lived through too many of them."

"Kit. Trace is here. She is out of stasis and doing fine. Good luck!"

Good news. Now to fulfill my end of the bargain.

I left the transport and groped my way through the airlock. Most airlocks were the same, and for years I could get through them with my eyes closed, and since I could not see, the familiarity was helpful.

On the opposite side, I stopped to get a sense of my surroundings. A piquant odor of pepper lingered in the air and the soft hum of the oxygen replenisher surrounded me on all sides. I tapped forward with my white cane, the traditional tool of the blind. For this occasion, however, the tip was sharpened to a point. A lethal weapon if I needed to use it.

I heard Neville's voice at the end of the hallway. It

grew louder as he approached, and I used the volume to time his arrival. I stopped before he reached me.

"Kit. I'm glad you could make it on your own. I understand that you are totally blind, now." There was a rush of air near my face. He must have tested the hypothesis by pulling a punch close to my eyes. I didn't move. "Very good. Let me help you."

He tried to take my arm to lead me forward, but I shrugged off his grip. I heard him grunt slightly, and he continued forward, ordering me to follow him. I tapped ahead a few more paces and totaled the number of steps in the hallway – a good practice to remember when in unfamiliar territory. We passed through a bulkhead into a more open space. The airflow was softer here and the sounds not as confined. I cleared my throat to try to get a read on if there was an echo. None, but that didn't tell me much.

I took a couple steps into the room when I felt Neville's presence next to me. His breath smelled like sour fruit. I tried to pull myself away from his new grip, but he turned me back to face him.

"So, you really can't see, huh?" My cheek was stung suddenly by a sharp slap. His grip was tighter, and he forced his words into my left ear. "That's for all the trouble you have caused me!"

I did some quick calculations. *If his face is here and the floor is here, then his groin should be just about – HERE.*

"Ooof! You bastard."

I was prepared for his return blow. I deflected it with my left forearm and grabbed his right shoulder as it passed by with my left hand. I then leveraged the cane and my right leg under his thigh and raised them both as high as I could. He fell to the floor with a grunt. I aimed the sharpened cane where I believed his throat had landed. I might have been off by a few centimeters. I might have pointed at his chest or between his eyes. It didn't matter. He got the point.

"Don't you know you should be kind to the blind!" I snarled. "Let's get on with this. There are people waiting for me."

I tapped away from him quickly before he could retaliate in some unseen manner. I heard a growl as he pushed his way back to his feet. He rushed up behind me and pushed me forward, making me lose count of the steps. He half lifted my body as we barreled forward and caused me to lose my balance. I began to fall forward, but Neville compensated for the motion and righted me before I toppled. Seconds later, I was dropped roughly into a slightly inclined leather chair. I heard the clatter of what may have been surgical instruments on a nearby table. I gritted my teeth and waited.

Something was placed on my head. I could feel needle sharp probes, but they did no more than prick as they touched my scalp. I felt warm rivulets of blood begin to trickle through my hair. I was apparently not going to receive the benefits of anesthesia or disinfectant.

"This will just take a minute. I want you to concentrate on an object which I will soon specify." It sounded as if he were reading a technical manual. "There will be a brief sensation of heat as the probes enter your skull. I will ask you a series of questions. Don't try to lie. I'll know immediately and you will be 'penalized'. Got that?"

"Get on with it!"

"Okay," he said with glee. "Here we go!"

I closed my eyes and braced for the worst. It really wasn't so bad after all. There was little pain – less than the beasties used to cause on a frequent basis. First, he started with basic questions: name, age, favorite color, favorite childhood experience, name of my first pet, date of my first gravball game. I felt the information being pulled to the front of my brain, complete with the minutest details – things I would have never remembered without some kind of help. Even the most distant memories seemed like they happened just minutes before.

Finally, he got to his big question: "Tell me about colonial crate number 52312d423 on *The Carthaginian*."

"What?!"

"You know what I'm talking about! I woke from stasis on *The Carthaginian* to find the cargo I put on board was gone. Then I learned that Trace was pregnant, a condition that would have been noted on the passenger manifest. I put two and two together. Trace woke early from stasis and ate the chocolate and got pregnant. But I guessed she had a little help, huh? The chocolates themselves did not get her pregnant, did they? I knew someone else was involved, and guessed correctly that it must've been the pilot. So, did you use the chocolate as an aphrodisiac?"

"No, she loved me unconditionally. The candy was a reward for both of us." It was an honest answer that was required by the parameters Neville had set up. I hadn't distracted him from his story, though.

"I knew you were involved. I mind-reamed Trace to find out what happened. She remembered a lot about her little encounter with you, but she didn't know where the crate went. She said that the two of you ate all of the contents of one of the crates. That's all I was able to learn from her. You smirched the ship's logs enough that it is impossible to determine what really transpired on board. I'm going to draw out the ingrained, subconscious memories and find that other crate of chocolate."

"This is about cargo? Not about making your fiancé pregnant."

"Understand, I'm not happy about that, but after all, I barely knew her. You may have ruined a wonderful life for me and my little wifey. I don't know. What I do know is that the chocolate could buy a planet. I want that crate."

"So you've been after me this whole time to satisfy your sweet tooth, not to seek revenge?"

"You don't get it, do you, Shicker?! I could care less about revenge. True, she is a juicy little morsel that I would have liked to have possessed, but that was long ago. I have more important concerns. One of economy. Of supply and demand. That crate is the only supply of chocolate left in the universe. The whole reeking universe! I could live comfortably on the sale of the crate alone, but I'm looking for more than that."

"That is the only chocolate left in the universe? I find that hard to believe."

"Believe. I've even been to Earth. I couldn't even get close to the planet. The reports from the environmentalists living there all say that it is too polluted to support life. No one is allowed in or out. So, there are no cocoa leaves. No candy bars. No bon bons, nothing."

"You can't realize how ridiculous you sound."

"And I don't care! The ridiculous has never been

worth so much! It's not my doing. It's supply and demand. And humans are literally dying for chocolate."

"I don't see it."

"It's simple. After humans left Earth, they left the last of the chocolate behind. It was deemed uncalled-for to pack candy in the supplies during The Last Evacuation. I was the only one that saw the possibilities and managed to get approval for one crate of chocolate on *The Carthaginian*. It was hardly enough, so I found away to get on a second one. I had incredible foresight. Once the colonies were established, Humanity got its sweet tooth back. The last few candy bars were eaten, but people longed for more and so far, we have yet to come up with a substitute for the sweets. I hope we never do –"

"One crate of chocolate is not going to go a long way."

"That's where you're wrong. We have molecular reproducers, now. Once I have a decent-sized sample, I will be able to grow my own supply of chocolate from sand. I'll have a corner on the market. I'll be richer than God!"

"Somehow, I don't think God is interested in being 'rich', but I guess that is beside the point, isn't it?"

"It is," he sniveled.

"You know, we ate one of those crates."

"I know, and I'm not very pleased about that. You realize that you ate a planet when you did that?"

"So that's what blew my diet."

"One crate is barely enough to get the molecular repros going, but it'll suffice. Now, you'll remember the time and the course of *The Carthaginian* when supply crate number 52312d423 was ejected. So concentrate on that crate, and we are finished."

I shook my head, not in disagreement, but in disbelief. The momentary pains caused by the movement brought me back to my senses and helped me to concentrate.

"Do you remember the crate listed on *The Carthaginian* as number 52312d423?" Neville demanded. He was more insistent now.

I didn't try to resist. "Yes."

"What did you do with it?"

Mechanically I said, "I ejected it into interstellar space."

"Haha! See this is fun! What was the mass of the crate?"

"Thirty kilograms."

"Plenty enough! This kind of money and I'll be free of The Old Man forever!"

He must not have heard of the latest happenings on The Hub. Not surprising. They were trying to keep the news of the Inner Sanctum explosion hushed to avoid a panic.

I tried to keep my answers short and specific, concentrating only on the one item of Neville's affection. I could feel memories being pulled from my mind, drawn out almost by magic. I recited dates, times, course trajectories all remembered from brief log entries and quick glances at the ship's clock. From these he would be able to determine where, in the infinite expanse of space, drifted a tiny, thirty-kilogram crate. In the end, he got the information that he wanted. It was information that I didn't mind giving to him.

It was soon over and the probes pulled out of my skull smoothly. There was little pain except for the trickle of blood that stung my eyes.

Neville was quickly back in my face again. I turned from his hot breath, but he grabbed me by the chin and forced me to look at him, as if my eyes still functioned.

"That wasn't so bad was it?" he laughed.

I answered with silence.

"Now we each have what we want. I'll be rich beyond the dreams of men, and you will have your little dream girl. I think I got the best of the deal."

I disagreed silently.

"Now for the last of the unfinished business. I promised to let you live, but I never said in what condition – "

He struck me several times in the face with his fists. I was helpless to defend myself but tried my best to ward off his blows with my arms. After a few seconds, the attack subsided and he backed away. My face bloated with pain, but I had expected worse.

"Any parting words?" he asked.

"Eat shit," I said through puffy lips.

"Frankly, I expected more. A pithy retort or snappy comeback, but that is all you can manage? How about 'I'm sorry?'"

"Eat shit," I repeated.

"Finc. I'll be leaving now. Not by the ship which I'm sure your father has targeted or booby trapped by now, but by a special little exit which I devised."

I remained silent as I heard an airlock somewhere cycle. I sat motionless as I heard the roar of thrusters push a modified bridge away from the ship. I stayed motionless a few minutes longer, feeling lucky to be alive and glad that finally the whole thing was over. I was free.

Free.

I reactivated the comlink.

"Dad, are you alright?"

"Not bad considering. I could use some help over here, though."

"We'll be right there. Neville is leaving. Do you want us to do anything?"

"No. Let him go. He thinks that he's bested me. Let it stay that way."

"Any parting message for him."

I tried to contain it, but I couldn't keep it inside of me any longer. I started to laugh like a madman. It was an uncontrollable cackle from deep within my soul. I made no effort to restrain it.

"Dad?"

"Tell him to 'EAT SHIT!'" I blurted between whoops.

I must have laughed for hours.

Chapter Nineteen

"It is so dark in here. I can't see a thing."

"Yes," I told Trace. "I wanted us to be on equal footing."

"But I want to see what you look like after all these years."

"I feel the same way."

Trace ran her hands along my body. "Yes," she giggled, "You do feel the same."

It was a bit clumsy, but we maneuvered each other to the bed, sharing a prolonged kiss along the way. Without exchanging a word, we undressed each other.

The memories Neville extracted helped to give me a clear picture of the woman I'd known ten years or so back on my timeline. A little more time had passed on Trace's, but not much. Now, I had to get to know her on a new level. I would make a mental map of her body. My hands had to relay a new picture of this woman whom I'd never stopped loving.

I began at the top, brushing my hands through her soft hair. I remembered that it was blond, and silky. It was longer than the shoulder length that I recalled, but the difference was insignificant. I mapped the contours of her face twice, picturing in my mind her large eyes and full, red cheeks. Her neck was still thin, and she shivered slightly as I traced the arc of her chin.

I moved lower. Her breasts were soft and her nipples grew hard in the palms of my hands. Then I felt the sharp edge of her rib cage and the solid base of her abdomen. I rustled through coarse hair and found soft, warm, moist velvet below. She moaned faintly.

She still had long, firm legs. I found the tips of her toes and then my cartographic tour ended. I was not disappointed. She was the same as the day I last saw her.

Then she began her exploration. It was awkward, but in a gentle way. She did not have the same experience without sight that I had, but she made a practical, methodical search. She began with the top of my head, proceeded down my face, neck, chest, and stomach. She delayed quite a bit when she moved further south. I didn't mind. She never made it to my toes.

We made love in a fury of passion. It was passion augmented by a love that had no depth and swallowed our souls. We were consumed by it and strengthened by it. We were one with amour. And with each other.

We had returned to paradise.

We lay silently for a long time. Later, she softly broke the stillness.

"You have changed," she said. "You're better than before."

"We'll see if you still feel the same way when we turn on the lights."

We had our choice of destinations, but few offered sanctuary, And we had two important stops to make on our way.

First, we unfolded in the Kozarian system. It was a possible hideout for us. E'Lowa had offered to let us settle there, but we declined. Too obvious to those who may be pursuing us. E'Lowa admitted that he was grateful and even admired the stand and sacrifice I'd made for his planet. He was even considering treating with Humans after all. That would have surprised The Old Man, although I suspect that the Human ruler's demise opened the door to talks far more than anything that I did.

Our objective in the system was the Human probe pointing toward the star. We correctly assumed that the probe was the key to whatever caused the nova. During periods of decline in nova activity, the probe would activate a mechanism that caused the flares. Claude had the idea of inserting a readout generator that would send the probe a false, but varying, interpretation of the sun's activity. The mechanism would never refire, and the Kozarians would eventually regain their sight. Then Kozar could destroy the probe, which was probably the source of the flares. As an added bonus, the Shoorulians would see the same readouts and never learn of the cessation of flares and would keep their distance.

We made one more stop in the middle of empty space and then entered orbit around a small blue planet that now stood at the very edge of Human space. Earth.

It was Neville who gave us the idea of settling there. His reports of a dead planet didn't seem correct. Claude's research proved that there was a small settlement of environmentalists on the planet. They warned off all who came by, stating that the planet was unlivable, yet there were never any supplies coming in

223

or out which meant the life was sustainable there. Which meant that we could live there.

So, we did.

Thanks, Neville.

Life there wasn't easy, but it wasn't exactly hard. The Earth was making a fantastic comeback, thanks to the scientists who came to "study" the effects and devastation inflicted on the planet by years of Human abuse. They found a planet well on the road back to recovery, but they realized how quickly that would be ruined if people returned, so they sent out regular reports of the ruinous condition of the planet and asked for the cooperation of the few who managed to settle there. So far, all have agreed.

Earth was much different than the planet from which the colonists fled. Life evolved quickly once the cause of environmental pollution (Humanity) was removed. The diversity of life never materialized like before, however. Most of the evolving forms seem to have come from dogs, birds, rats, and cockroaches, but they have improved from the originals. We missed some life which has become extinct, however – most of all the large sea mammals. We regretted that the porpoises and whales are gone forever.

Trace built a wonderful home for us on a warm and sunny wooded beach. Her survivalist skills and pioneering spirit made every day full of gratifying hard work and adventure. Even Zachary was able to curb his wanderlust and make family life a reality. On those days when he became too unsettled, he just entered the woods for a time. We never worried about him. There were no large predators left on Earth. After a few days, he would return and the family would be together again.

One day Walt appeared. He reported that

Humanity was poised on the brink of a new age. There was only one Old Man left, and his health was failing. Colonists were learning on their own how to cooperate and survive.

Self-determination was on the way.

In a brief aside, he offered me my sight back. He had the knowledge and the tools to implant the beasties. I wasn't ready for it, so I declined. He also offered me a pair of Kozarian optics. I wasn't even ready for that. For the time being, I was happy to experience the lush growth and wildlife that was growing around us.

Walt explained how he was able to follow us, using a homing mechanism built into the cloning process. "You almost lost me, though. You made a funny stop after leaving Kozar. I flew right past you before I realized it."

"Sorry, it was necessary." I explained the business with Neville.

"But you gave him the coordinates of the crate of chocolate, right?"

"Well, yes. The crate. That's what he asked for, but I had used 'the crate' to account for the waste from our sanitary facility. He never asked what was in it. It wasn't full of chocolate."

"Oh, shit!" he laughed.

"Exactly."

"So why the extra stop."

"Days before I changed trajectory and ejected the crate from *The Carthaginian*, I had ejected contraband from the ship. Another identical crate, but not case number 52312d423. It was illegal contraband with an illegal number on the manifest. I firmly established that in my mind before he questioned me. Neville didn't think to ask about it. After he did his mind ream, I asked Claude to do a new one, this time to get information on the first crate. The one full of chocolate."

"So, in the end, there is a lesson to this whole business."

"Dare I suggest it has something to do with 'just desserts'?"

Walt snorted with disdain, "You daren't."

"Have it you way."

The sun was getting hot as noon approached, so I moved three steps northwest into the shade of our cabin. Walt declined to follow me. He was enjoying his days in the sun after working most of his days in the freezing environment of the regen chambers.

"So, you have the chocolate, right? You're rich? That's what you're telling me?"

I shrugged. "Wealth is such a relative thing."

"Well, you may need it. That's one of the reasons I came here. People have found out about the homing mechanism. And there are people who are interested in finding you. You may need the money to keep them at bay."

Again, I shrugged. "I've never had to look for adventure. It always seems to find me."

"You can't just wait for them to pounce on you."

"I'm enjoying myself, now. I'll think I'll stay right here. I am ready. If they pounce, then I'll fight. I've always been a great counterpouncer."

"I'm telling you, they are already on their way. What are you going to do?"

I tapped my way over to the side of our thatched hut. I could hear Trace singing to herself inside. I opened a small refrigerator unit and removed a handful of nuggets. I offered one to Walt.

"I think I'll have another piece of chocolate," I answered.

Sonny Wareham is an author and screenwriter who lives in the suburbs of Chicago. He looks forward to the future.